GirlForce

To the GirlForce girls—Aura-Lea Withers, Eloise Winestock, Alexandra Arakie, Jessica Harrison, and Isabella Jacob—thanks for your inspiration.

First published in Australia in 2004 by ABC Books for the Australian Broadcasting Corporation
Published in the United States in 2009 by Bloomsbury U.S.A. Children's Books
175 Fifth Avenue, New York, New York 10010

Library of Congress Cataloging-in-Publication Data
Goldstein, Nikki.
Girlforce / By Nikki Goldstein. — 1st U.S. ed.
p.   cm.
ISBN-13: 978-1-59990-389-7 • ISBN-10: 1-59990-389-X (hardcover)
ISBN-13: 978-1-59990-354-5 • ISBN-10: 1-59990-354-7 (paperback)
1. Women—Health and hygiene. 2. Somatotypes. I. Title.
RA778.G686 2009   613'.04244—dc22   2008038277

First U.S. Edition 2009
Printed in China
(hardcover) 10 9 8 7 6 5 4 3 2 1
(paperback) 10 9 8 7 6 5 4 3 2 1

All papers used by Bloomsbury U.S.A. are natural, recyclable products made from wood grown in
well-managed forests. The manufacturing processes conform to the environmental regulations of the
country of origin.

Edited by Jody Lee
Designed by Greendot Design Pty Ltd
Photographs by Prue Ruscoe (except as noted below)
Flower and yoga illustrations by Anna Augul
Color reproduction by PageSet, Melbourne

Additional picture credits
Page 57: Jupiter Images/i2i/Alamy
Page 70: Pixland/Photolibrary
Page 77: Blend Images/Alamy
Page 107: Polka Dot Images/Jupiter Images
Page 142: Digital Vision/Photolibrary
Page 185, top: Banana Stock/Photolibrary

A Girl's
Guide to
the Body
and Soul

GirlForce

Nikki
Goldstein

BLOOMSBURY

NEW YORK BERLIN LONDON

GirlForce Starts Here! 07

Chapter One Who Are You? 10

Chapter Two Create Your Own GirlForce
Body Type Balancing Plan 29

Chapter Three Eat Right for Your Body Type 39

contents

Chapter Four DIY Body Blast 71

Chapter Five Celebrate Your Unique Beauty 106

Chapter Six The Lowdown on Stress 140

Chapter Seven Get in Touch with Your Inner Self 167

Chapter Eight Talking about Relationships 187

Chapter Nine Get It Together 202

Chapter Ten Your GirlForce Questions Answered 215

GirlForce
Starts Here!

Hi Everyone,

Ever wondered why you can stay up late and party while your best friend is ready to crash? Or why you have curvy hips and a butt while your classmates are X-rays? I did, until I discovered Ayurveda, the ancient medical system of India. According to Ayurveda (which has been around for about 5,000 years and is pronounced eye-ur-vay-dah), everyone has a unique Body Type made up of the elements Air, Fire, and Earth. When you tap into the elemental-energies that dominate your body and mind, you'll be destined for a happy, healthy, and balanced life. Sound good?

   I discovered Ayurveda after a long illness that sent me down for the count. (I nearly died.) As I began the long, slow process of recovery, a friend recommended I try yoga and meditation. At first I was like, "Yeah, how will making like a pretzel help me?" But once I got into it, I discovered that yoga made me feel strong and vital, and meditation helped me chill out. It really helped.

Not many people know this, but both yoga and meditation are branches of Ayurveda. Ayurveda offers a complete system for living. The basic idea is that we humans are part of nature, and we contain elements of nature: Air (in the lungs and mind); Fire (in the blood and metabolism); and Earth (in the bones, tissues, and structure of the body). Ayurveda also offers the idea that one of those elements (I call them elemental-energies) dominates your body and mind. Whichever elemental-energy is strongest within you gives you your mental, physical, and spiritual characteristics—in other words, your Body Type.

Your Body Type is the key to a secret inner world of feelings, desires, passions, and ideas. It predisposes you to certain physical and mental traits: Air Types are generally thin and creative; Fire Types are mostly passionate and athletic; and Earth Types are often curvy and laid-back. I like to think of the Body Types as archetypes, like your star sign. And just like your star sign, there will be characteristics you can relate to and some that you think don't apply, because everyone's different, unique, one-of-a-kind.

And the best news yet about **GirlForce** is that you don't have to be any particular shape or size, color or race to get the good vibes. **GirlForce** does not discriminate in any way—in fact, it's the opposite. When you tune into the force for good within you, you begin to accept yourself and others unconditionally. You cease negative self-talk and you stop judging others. **GirlForce** helps you connect with the part of yourself that is like everyone else, your spirit or life energy. In learning to live in harmony with my Body Type, I've also discovered how to live in harmony with nature. And that has been awesome. When you live in harmony with nature, you feel connected to everything and everyone. It's the best spiritual high you can get.

Which leads me to explain my concept of **GirlForce** . . .

Getting in touch with the **GirlForce** within is a spiritual experience. It's not about joining a religious sect or believing in anything—except **yourself**. When you're in touch with nature, you are, in fact, connecting to your own spirit or **GirlForce**—the power within that makes you who you are.

When you consciously balance your Body Type every day with healing and balancing practices such as yoga, meditation, eating, and exercising right for your Body Type, pampering for your Body Type, even dressing for your Body Type—you unleash the power of **GirlForce**. Cool, huh? Think of it like this: every time you do something nurturing for yourself, you're having a spiritual experience and you're connecting to the power of **GirlForce**.

The only way to really understand **GirlForce** is to feel it. And there are a million ways you can feel it (in fact, you already have), like taking a walk outside with your best friend and taking in the smell of nature and the feel of the sun on your skin, like slurping a cup of hot chocolate on a cold day, like doing something kind for a friend, or like laughing with someone you love . . . Because **GirlForce** is already within you, you feel it all the time even though you've probably never labeled it.

GirlForce has changed my life for the better. I now know there's a force inside me that not only connects me to nature but gives me the best natural high imaginable. **GirlForce** gives me confidence and helps me accept myself—just the way I am. Get into **GirlForce**. It's so sweet!

Love,

As I mentioned in my letter, I used Ayurveda, meditation, and yoga to heal myself and work toward a greater sense of harmony and well-being. For the purposes of this book, I have used Ayurveda and its body typing system, but it's important for you to realize there are many different ways to classify body types—Ayurveda is just one way. I also want you to know that it's possible you will not fit neatly into one Body Type—don't worry, you'll still get a lot out of using this book. The idea is to use **GirlForce** as a way to open your mind and have fun.

CHAPTER ONE

Who Are You?

What is GirlForce? GirlForce is girl power. **GirlForce** is love. **GirlForce** is vitality. **GirlForce** is beauty. **GirlForce** is compassion. **GirlForce** is energy. **GirlForce** is fun. **GirlForce** is growth. **GirlForce** is nature. **GirlForce** is magic. **GirlForce** is YOU.

Which Body Type Are You?

Fire

Air

Earth

Get ready for it. You're about to go on an awesome ride. You're going to discover the secrets of who you are and who you can be. GirlForce is your key to feeling totally strong, fabulous, and cool. When you dive into this book and discover how to tap into this unlimited power source—your GirlForce—you'll never look back.

Air, Fire, Earth— learn to love your Body Type and you're on your way to feeling good.

READY TO GET INTO THE GIRLFORCE mind and body blitz? Here is the ultimate guide to looking and feeling amazing inside and out so you can make the most of what you've got.

You're about to find out whether you're a creative and adventurous Air babe; a hot and sultry Fire chick; or a cool, calm, and collected Earth angel. Your Body Type is your secret doorway to the source of your power and your long-term happiness, health, and well-being.

Figuring out your Body Type will take you on a journey into a new world of experience and awareness. It gives you profound insights into your deeper self, and once you know which elemental-energies affect your moods, body shape, skin tone and texture, spiritual tendencies, tastes and desires, you'll discover heaps of info and know-how. When you get a handle (which won't take you long) on how different Body Types think and act, you'll know so much about yourself and your friends and family that you'll amaze everyone. Blow them away with all the secret stuff you've figured out about them.

There's another thing you need to know. Your Body Type is a gift from nature and is fueled by the loving and vital energy I call GirlForce. Think of it like this: your body and mind and their unique traits are like a car with its hip exterior, cool interior, and engine. GirlForce is the gas that makes the car go. You can take care of the car, polishing it regularly and filling it with the right kind of fuel, or you can neglect it, let it rust, and run it into the ground. One of the main principles of GirlForce is that your choices about the way you live your life have long-term ramifications.

Like a hot racing car, your Body Type is your vehicle through life. GirlForce is the fuel.

The truth is, it takes a long time to run your body into the ground. But the present is always the best time to establish healthy habits that will sustain and support you for the rest of your life.

GirlForce is about helping you discover the joys of your unique self. Learning to love your Body Type—JUST AS IT IS—is one of the first steps on your path to self-love. Connecting to GirlForce, the power within, is a major buzz. Nothing feels as good as being filled with the energy of life. It's free and it sure beats spending all your cash on alcohol or drugs. It's totally empowering.

The GirlForce Body Type Quiz

Here it is! Your entry card to a new world of experience and fun. This easy quiz will reveal your Body Type. And once you know your Body Type, you will be able to get into all the great GirlForce remedies, recipes, therapies, and programs.

The quiz is divided into two sections, "Body" and "Mind," with ten questions for each one. As you go through the test, circle the answer that most closely resembles you—a, b, or c. Only circle one answer per question, even if you feel you fall somewhere between two answers. Take your time to consider the qualities mentioned in the quiz and treat it as a cool learning experience.

How to Score

At the end of each section, add up the number of a's, b's, and c's. **The highest number of a's, b's, or c's should reveal your Body Type and indicate the dominant elemental-energy in your constitution—in other words, you'll discover whether you're an Air, Fire, or Earth Body Type!** Even if the scores are really close, the number of a's, b's, or c's that has the highest score will reveal your dominant elemental-energy—and your Body Type.

Most people are dominated by one elemental-energy—Air, Fire, or Earth. It is possible that you may have scored an equal number across two or three elemental-energies. If you're unsure which Body Type you are, read through all the information about the three different Body Types (further on in this chapter, and check out the Personality Profiles in Chapter Seven), and you'll find you relate to one more strongly than the others.

1. How would you describe your body frame?

a) Slim with a small frame, either very tall or petite.

b) Medium frame with good muscle definition.

c) Solid or curvaceous frame; can gain weight easily.

2. How would you describe your skin?

a) My skin is prone to dryness, and even compared to other people of my race, I'm considered dark-skinned.

b) My skin is sensitive, prone to breakouts, burns easily, has reddish undertones, and is warm to the touch.

c) My skin is oily, thick, and pale for my race. It's cool to the touch.

3. How would you describe your hair?

a) My hair is wavy or kinky, dark or light. I'd like it to be thicker.

b) My hair is soft, blonde, red, or brunette with red highlights.

c) My hair is thick, dark brown, or dark blonde and lustrous.

4. How much energy do you have?

a) It comes and goes in high-energy bursts, and I burn out quickly.

b) I have loads of energy, but if I'm tired, I'm looking for the nearest bed.

c) I have good stamina, but I don't like to be budged if I'm chilling on the couch.

5. How are your zzzzz's?

a) I sleep very lightly and have lots of dreams, sometimes waking during the night.

b) I sleep soundly, but when I'm awake, I'm awake.

c) I sleep deep and long.

6. What's your relationship to food?

a) I don't have a strong appetite. Sometimes I forget to eat.

b) I can't live without food. If I don't eat on time I get cranky.

c) I love food, but I'm rarely starving.

A's = 5 B's = 2 C's = 3

7. How's your thirst quotient?

a) I don't crave liquids, but I will drink if something's put in front of me.

b) Ohmigod, give me a drink, I'm parched.

c) I sometimes have to remind myself to drink.

8. What's your response to the weather?

a) I hate the cold, especially on windy days.

b) Hot days burn me up.

c) Cold, damp conditions make me depressed.

9. How do you rate yourself as an athlete?

a) I'm flexible and agile, but I can't hack a long gym class.

b) I'm athletic and strong, and I enjoy the competition.

c) I can last the distance, but I'm rarely that motivated to exercise.

10. When you exert yourself, what happens?

a) I tire easily, sweat a little bit, and feel exhausted if I overdo it.

b) If I go hard at it, I sweat a lot, feel energized, and then need to rest.

c) I am slow to start and will perspire a bit, but after a good workout I feel uplifted.

1. Which words best describe you?
a) Adventurous, curious, original, exciting, charming
b) Passionate, challenging, stimulating, powerful
c) Stable, kind, deep, faithful, serene, compassionate

2. Which words best describe your talents?
a) Innovative and creative
b) Good leader and decision maker
c) Nurturing and imaginative

3. How would you describe your memory?
a) Poor long-term
b) Good, quick, sharp
c) Good retention

4. You long for?
a) Independence, change, spontaneity
b) Challenge, pleasure, competition
c) Pleasing others, security

5. The thing you most value is?
a) Integrity
b) Honesty
c) Compassion

6. The things you fear are?
a) Confinement, boredom, too much routine
b) Slowness, not getting on with stuff
c) Change and loss

7. When you're stressed out, are you . . .
a) Anxious
b) Aggressive
c) Withdrawn

8. Your approach to homework could be described as . . .
a) Creative, innovative, flexible
b) Intellectual, problem solving, goal-oriented
c) Diligent yet relaxed

A's=3 B's=4 C's=3

all together

A's=8 B's=6 C's=6

9. The way you handle money is . . .

a) Spendthrift, literally slips through my fingers.

b) I like to spend on luxuries, but otherwise I'm quite conscious of how I spend my pennies.

c) Careful, I like to save money.

10. How would your friends describe you?

a) Sentimental, sensitive, eccentric

b) Passionate, loyal, intense, sometimes demanding

c) Loving, forgiving, a good listener

One great way to do the GirlForce Body Type Quiz is to share the experience with someone else. Whether you do it with your BFF or a group of friends, you'll get great insights into yourself and the people around you if you discuss the questions and work out the answers together.

Air, Fire, and Earth: The Awesome GirlForce Body Types

Welcome to the GirlForce universe! You're about to get a whole lot wiser about yourself and your friends and family.

Once you understand the different traits and qualities of the elemental-energies Air, Fire, and Earth, you'll see how they "flavor" people's physical, mental, and emotional lives and how they operate in yourself and in others.

You'll get amazing insights into the weird and wacky parts of yourself, like why you hate the cold or love to spend money. You'll become aware of the wonderful, unique traits and qualities that make you YOU and develop compassion for the parts of your nature that are sometimes vulnerable and testy.

air fire
earth

Air

Fire

Earth

Mostly a's
I'm an Air girl

Outgoing Air girls make friends easily because they love to talk, flirt, and entertain their friends. They're spontaneous and unpredictable and often up for a challenge. Air girls are witty, enthusiastic, creative, always on the go, energetic, and quick to learn. When they're stressed, they get nervous and anxious. Because they're light sleepers with irregular hunger patterns, if you catch them after a few late nights of watching reruns or a couple of skipped meals, they'll be total air-heads. They hate routine and crave constant change and excitement. And because of their naturally quick minds, they're often bored at school and fantasize about life after the bell rings. They make interesting, intuitive, and caring friends but they need a lot of space to exercise their eccentricities.

Positive traits: Imaginative and quick-witted, you are a natural-born inventor and innovator. You could be a fashion designer or an astrophysicist—whatever takes your fancy.

Your challenge: Too much to do, so little time . . . You get stressed, scattered, and exhausted because you're hopeless with routine.

You need: Time to indulge all your wild and wacky ideas—one day you will be discovered for your brilliance! In the meantime, get yourself together and give yourself some structure to work with. Slow down, breathe, and stop worrying.

Body Type Snapshot

Air girls are either very tall and slim (think string bean, like Gwyneth Paltrow or Taylor Momsen) or short and petite like Ashley Olsen, Jessica Alba, and Jada Pinkett-Smith. You often forget to eat, and you lose weight if you're stressed out. You're not a deep sleeper and loud noises, strong winds, and scary movies can keep you awake. You sometimes notice that your hands and feet are cold, and you long for the sensation of warmth on your skin. Speaking of skin, yours is often dry and craves a soothing moisturizer or body balm. Air girls are not overly fond of exercise. You tire easily and often stress that your knobby knees and elbows stick out of your gym clothes. For most Air girls, your hair is kinky and thin and the bane of your existence. You're the speedy, chatty, quirky girl in your posse.

Air

Mostly b's
I'm a Fire girl

Fire vixens are born leaders. They're intelligent, passionate, outgoing, confident about their abilities, and often highly competitive. You'll never have a dull moment with a Fire girl: she'll take control and bring wonder and excitement to the day because she's able to bring everyone together and inspire them to take part in her vision of fun and adventure. Be warned: they get hot under the collar easily and are often too proud to admit when they've made a mistake. Don't expect your Fiery gal pal to be sensitive to your needs; she's too busy trying to run the world to worry about your problems. That said, she's a friend indeed when you're a friend in need. She's loyal, funny, and always has a brilliant solution for your angst at her fingertips—give her a big-picture problem, and she'll effortlessly rise to the challenge. Fire girls are great organizers and make terrific team leaders—just remember to salute when she gives you an order.

Positive traits: You make everyone's party list because you're dynamic, passionate, and magnetic.

Your challenge: You're not always right, you know! It's a virtue to be a good loser, and you need to let others share some of the limelight.

You need: Spoil yourself occasionally and give yourself time to cool down and chill out. You're so busy marching to the finish line that sometimes you forget to stop and smell the roses. It's tough sometimes being fabulous—let yourself have a bad hair day every once in a while.

Fire

Body Type Snapshot

Fire girls are medium-sized and have strong bodies, like Rihanna, Reese Witherspoon, and Hilary Duff. You can put on and take off weight pretty easily and are naturally athletic. You tend to overheat in summer, and your skin burns easily. Fire gals are often identified by their soft blonde or reddish hair, and even when your hair is chocolate brown, it glints gold in the sunlight. Natural redheads like Lindsay Lohan and Nicole Kidman have made their glossy locks a major part of their signature style. You're the bossy one in your group, and your intensity and commitment to a cause distinguishes you from your Air and Earth girlfriends. Fire girls get grumpy when they're hungry (so don't keep them waiting), and they have a wicked sweet tooth. If you blush easily, you're likely to be a passionate Fire babe.

Earth

Body Type Snapshot

Earth girls are curvaceous and laid-back, like Liv Tyler and Beyoncé Knowles, with large eyes, voluptuous lips, and sparkling white teeth. You tend to put on weight easily, especially around the hips and butt. Your skin is often pale for your race and can be a little oily, and your hair is most likely thick and lush. Mornings are not your favorite time of the day. You're a night owl, picking up momentum as the day goes on. Your eyes are your most prominent feature, and they sparkle with delight when you gaze at the people you love. You're not a fast talker, but people listen when you speak. You're the easygoing girl in your group, and your perceptive insights often blow everyone away.

Mostly c's
I'm an Earth girl

Earth babes are kind, family-minded, stable, calm, and serene. They'll never be two-faced (they won't steal your man or spill all your deep, dark secrets). Earth gals are dreamy, laid-back, and generous, and while they're not normally the girls who rush for the spotlight, their easygoing natures make them friends for life. They're affectionate and forgiving, but if you wound them they'll bear a grudge because they can hold on to things for a long time. Earth girls have a tendency to procrastinate, and at their worst, they're couch potatoes who are resistant to change and movement. Earth girls need stimulation, so these Types thrive when they're challenged and excited. One thing that always gives Earth girls away: they're great at dispensing advice, so tap them for hints on how to tame your difficult boyfriend or bothersome brothers and sisters. Earth girls are naturally sensuous and loving, and their innate sense of beauty and harmony make them total style queens.

Positive traits: You're always the one everyone depends on in a crisis. You're a devoted friend who brings balance to any relationship.

Your challenge: When you let yourself go, you end up lazy. You must not give in to your laid-back nature to the degree that you become tired and lackluster.

You need: You're so busy being everyone's best friend you can forget about yourself. Treat yourself to a yummy facial or a walk outside every week. Time alone is a must. At the same time, stimulation and challenge will prevent you from getting into a rut. Give yourself an energy injection every day.

Welcome to the GirlForce World

Congratulations, you've discovered your Body Type. Your Body Type is your passport to unlocking the awesome powers of GirlForce. When you nurture your Body Type with the right foods, exercises, meditations, yoga moves, clothes, colors, essential oils, and jewelry, your whole being vibrates with energy and power. Now that you know who you are (Air, Fire, or Earth—or a unique and incredible combination of two or three of the elemental-energies), you'll be able to design a lifestyle plan that will unleash your full potential with practical ways to turn up the volume on your inner strength. The following chapters give you a step-by-step guide to high-voltage confidence and an awesome life. Ready to learn more? Read on!

CHAPTER TWO

Create Your Own GirlForce Body Type Balancing Plan

Wanna feel amazing every day? It's all about balance. Get in touch with your inner self—your GirlForce—then rest, eat, and play to suit your Body Type.

Here are your instructions: **1. Have fun. 2. Have more fun. 3.** Let go of all your preconceived ideas about what it means to be healthy and full of life—GirlForce sets a new benchmark. **4.** Read the whole book before you set out your plan. **5.** You'll get more out of the GirlForce philosophy if you read stuff about the other Body Types, not just your own. That way you'll discover loads of info about your friends and family. **6.** Don't beat yourself up—about anything. **7.** Work it, girl! The more you put in, the more you'll get out. **8.** Share what you discover with your friends—you'll spread the positive GirlForce vibes. **9.** Go with the flow; don't stress. **10.** Rome wasn't built in a day; be gentle with yourself and make any changes at your own pace. Simple, huh?

Connect to the GirlForce Within

From now on you're going to be a self-healing expert. GirlForce is a DIY self-pampering, self-nurturing, self-healing program that gives you the power to choose a healthy way to live and be. Sweet!

No one knows your body like you do. So it stands to reason that the person who should be responsible for its upkeep and maintenance is you. Yup, you're in the driver's seat. Being in the driver's seat comes with some challenges. You have to be aware of the road (your life), you have to be alert for traffic lights (moments when you need to stop, slow down, or go on ahead), and you have to make sure you don't fall asleep at the wheel or trash yourself too much on the way to the party (both unsafe practices on the road to growing up).

Every chapter gives you a piece of the GirlForce Body Type Balancing Plan, from eating right for your Type, great yoga moves, beauty, dealing with stress, why you act the way you do, and relationships to answers for those embarrassing questions you were too afraid to ask. Put all of this together and you have a balancing plan that gives you amazing girl power!

Love Your Body Type

Now is a good time to explain a little more about the relationship between GirlForce and your Body Type.

Your Body Type is a perfect expression of nature. And as a part of nature (and wooohooo, nature is a chick-energy, as in Mother Nature) we are all made up of the elemental-energies—Air, Fire, and Earth. In most of us **one of these elements dominates—we call the dominant element your Body Type** (even if it only dominates your scores by one or two points) because it largely flavors and colors your physical, emotional, and spiritual traits. Ayurvedic Body Typing won't work for everyone, but this 5,000-year-old art and science maintains that your Body Type doesn't just describe the way you look, it influences the way you act and feel.

I've called the three basic Body Types Air, Fire, and Earth because we can relate to those archetypes. For example, we all have girlfriends who are Air Types. They're the air-heads of the class. Inspired and creative yet sometimes vague and out there, they're always late, they often lose things, they're occasionally nervy, and exceptionally worried at exam time. Likewise, we all know Fire Types. They're the born leaders who can rally anyone to join their cause. They're often keen athletes who like to win, and they can get hot under the collar if you don't agree with them. They can be bossy, but they're also magnetic and charming and make passionate and devoted friends and partners. And finally, we all have friends who are Earth girls. They're solid and grounded. They like to nurture (so you probably confide in them a lot), and they're the ones who regularly want to skip gym class. Their motto is slow and steady wins the race.

When you balance your Body Type with foods, exercise, meditation, and yoga and clothes, colors, jewelry, and beauty treatments that are right for your Type—GirlForce flows. It's as simple as that!

When you connect to the Force and work it, you'll look and feel awesome.

The reason you feel confident when you tap into **GirlForce** is because **GirlForce** is a force of Nature herself.

GirlForce is a celebration of your unique self. It's like a battery inside that never runs out. It's your girl power source and the energy that drives your body, mind, and spirit.

One of the clearest ways GirlForce manifests in you is confidence. Right now you're probably thinking, "How can I be confident when I've got zits, a bulging butt, or flagging grades?" But what if you knew you could develop earth-shattering confidence, unbeatable self-esteem, tease-proof self-trust just by tapping into GirlForce? You'd be like, "Where can I get it?" The good news is that GirlForce exists within each and every one of us, and when you work with the tools and techniques in this book, you'll get a grip on it in next to no time.

You don't have to be the most popular girl in school or the best looking to have a full, "at the ready" supply of GirlForce as it's beyond the external things in your life. It transcends cellulite, bad hair days, and peer pressure. It's knowing inside you're more than how you look, think, or feel. GirlForce is the deep sense within that you're a part of nature, the universe, divine love—whatever you want to call it. And as part of nature, you're perfect. When you trust the beauty and power of nature, you also trust yourself.

Okay, so it sounds a little cosmic. But when you sit for a minute and think about the connection between the trees and plants, the oceans, the animals on the planet, the stars in the sky, and ourselves, you'll notice that we're all made up of the same stuff: carbon, oxygen, water, and minerals. You don't have to be a scientist to get that we're all part of a great continuum of life, expressed in each of us as our individual bodies, minds, and spirits. GirlForce gives you the understanding that you can celebrate your unique body, mind, and spirit *because* it's a beautiful expression of nature and universal love.

This book is designed to help you understand that, as an expression of nature, your body, mind, and spirit are magical, unique, and worthy of love—especially self-love. When you love yourself, unconditionally, you can withstand the highs and lows of life: getting dumped by your latest boyfriend or girlfriend, freaking out at exam time, fighting with your friends, or being misunderstood by your parents and teachers.

And guess what? You can use the mega-powers of GirlForce for your own health and well-being. When you connect to the Force and work it, you'll look and feel awesome!

You have the power to increase GirlForce in your body, mind, and spirit, and you also have the power to decrease its flow. The choices you make in your life alter the current of GirlForce; like a radio where you can turn up the volume or turn it right down, you have the power to juice up your body, mind, and spirit or send them down into the dumps.

It's kinda obvious really. Partying hard and smoking is one way to turn your GirlForce down, while going for a walk with your best friend is an activity that will send your GirlForce sky high. This is not about guilting you for going wild every now and again, it's just about being aware that your lifestyle choices have big implications when it comes to your vital energy.

All the info that follows gives you all the tools you need to get connected to your inner power and balance your Body Type.

Don't worry if you don't feel you fit into one Body Type EXACTLY. The Body Type lifestyle plans are designed to be suggestions not rules, and they're also meant to be flexible so you can tailor-make them for YOUR life and YOUR needs. And remember, we all have the elemental-energies Air, Fire, and Earth within us, so the key is to read everything about all the three different Body Types and borrow the bits and pieces that relate to YOU.

You'll discover that GirlForce is precious and needs to be nurtured. It's possible to squander your reserves of this vital energy, so take care of yourself: you're precious and special and there's no one like you on the planet.

So get with the plan and connect with your GirlForce!

CHAPTER THREE

Eat Right for Your Body Type

Listen up. Your body needs the **right** kind of **fuel** to go the distance. Here's everything **you need** to **munch** on so you can keep your energy high.

In terms of food, there's no such thing as one size fits all. Foods that balance your Body Type aren't necessarily right for your best friend and vice versa. Each Body Type benefits from specific foods that help increase your levels of energy and GirlForce. Find out which foods are right for your Body Type. You'll learn healthy eating habits that will keep you in tip-top shape. Yum!

IF YOU'RE CONFUSED ABOUT WHAT TO EAT and which diet to follow, you're not alone. Every time we turn on the TV or read a magazine we're told something different about what to put in our mouths. This gorgeous, outrageously beautiful celebrity follows the protein diet, that super-rich singer only eats fruit. If you followed all this advice to the letter you'd be bouncing from one fad diet to the next: your weight would be all over the place, your skin would break out, and your energy would hit rock bottom. It seems we need a better, safer, healthier way to eat and live than the crazy diets we see in the media.

Food is one of life's great pleasures, and it should be enjoyed on a daily basis. In our society there is way too much emphasis on the way we look rather than how healthy and strong we feel. Food is one of the essential building blocks of life, and it's also a powerful source of GirlForce. When you eat a diet that's filled with nature's bounty—one that includes fresh fruits, veggies, nuts, seeds, herbs, spices, meats, and dairy foods—your body literally hums with energy and vitality.

Being healthy, vibed, and empowered with the buzz of GirlForce is your key to feeling good about yourself and your life, no matter what shape or size you are. Eating according to your Body Type plugs you straight into GirlForce. You'll discover that the practice of eating right for your Type is not only fun and interesting, it's a positive high to do something health-giving, life-affirming, and Body Type balancing every day.

This chapter is more than simply a guideline to what to eat—it's a meditation on food. My aim is for you to be able to use food as a starting point to develop awareness of yourself and your Body Type. Because food gives you an immediate insight into your cravings, tastes, and desires, it shows you who you are.

As you go along, you'll discover that Air girls are not that interested in food and can easily pass up the ice cream that Fire Types will kill for. You'll find that Earth girls, who like to munch, benefit from light foods such as salads, and that Fire Types get grumpy when they're forced to skip a meal.

Sometimes eating right for your Body Type will mean that your skin will improve. Fire girls, who are often prone to zits, will find that their complexions become less fiery and aggravated when they add cooling foods, such as watermelon, to their menus. Sometimes eating right for your Body Type will mean you'll lose a little weight (although that's not the only reason to eat right for your Type). Earth girls often find they shed a few pounds when they cut down on oily foods. And sometimes you'll find that eating right for your Type means you feel calmer and less stressed. No matter what Body Type you are, eating right for your Body Type is a way of becoming more aware of your needs and your choices, and it's a way to balance your body and mind.

Eating right for your Body Type isn't about slimming down so you can impress a new crush or starving yourself to squeeze into a bikini. It's a new, fun, flexible way to eat and live that's designed to unleash the power of GirlForce. When you put the right foods into your body, you'll stave off cravings and balance your energy, stamina, and moods.

Where Do I Begin?

We all know that lounging on the couch eating pizza, guzzling soft drinks, and munching on chips isn't good for your body, let alone your soul. But because we're human, and imperfect, we often ignore the advice of doctors, moms, and magazines and stuff ourselves with junk food. In small doses, there's nothing wrong with eating junk, but problems occur when we make a habit of eating processed foods and fast foods because the body has to make do with limited nutritional reserves. It's like trying to fly to Mars with only enough gas to get you to the moon. Over time a poor diet translates into poor health and a depleted GirlForce.

Maybe you're thinking, "Yes, I want to eat well, I want to be healthy. But how do I do it?" And with fad diets on the market that encourage *Survivor*-style starvation, carb-burning, and protein-loading, you're right to be confused. The good news is that there is a system, one that's been in use for more than 5,000 years, which can help you design a simple, fun, delicious nutritional plan that will boost your energy and pump up the volume on your health and well-being. Ayurveda shows you how to eat for your Body Type and boost your GirlForce.

Food Is a Healing Force

Get this now! Dieting is bad for your body. It can cause weight gain, unhealthy weight loss, depression, poor concentration, zits, stress, and a bucket of other nasty symptoms. This chapter is NOT about going on a diet. In fact, the Nutritional Balancing Guides do away with dieting forever. You won't be asked to give up your favorite foods (and yup, that includes chocolate), or be directed to do anything that involves sticking to stressful routines or counting calories. What you will find are lists of foods,

drinks, herbs and spices, as well as dietary suggestions that will balance your particular Body Type to increase the power of GirlForce in your body, mind, and spirit.

The idea is that once you tune into your Body Type, when you discover its natural likes and dislikes, you will be able to adapt the Nutritional Balancing Guide to suit your tastes, desires, and appetite. From meal to meal and from day to day you will be able to select from a wide variety of fresh fruits, vegetables, meats, seeds, oils, nuts, dairy products, herbs, spices, and drinks and design menus that suit. You can adapt the food selections for your specific tastes and lifestyle as well as your cultural heritage. The food groups are in lists so you can eat Italian, Chinese, Mexican, Japanese, Lebanese, Indian, or any other cuisine that takes your fancy whenever you like. Cool, huh?

What this system really offers is a way to simplify your choices. Its tried and tested ancient wisdom gives you the opportunity to introduce new tastes, textures, and menus when you feel like it. The idea is not to offer a "quick fix" or a "blanket solution" to every dietary need under the sun. The nutritional suggestions are a starting point. And as you become more aware of the foods that are prescribed for your Body Type, you will be able to adapt those foods to the changes in your life and lifestyle. You will also notice there are many foods you are already naturally and effortlessly attracted to. In time you will come to understand that these foods are also the foods that help provide the foundations of good health.

The more you include Body Type balancing foods and menus into your daily life, the faster you'll see results. Your body will thank you for the care you take with your diet and will reward you by naturally letting go of many of the foods and substances that imbalance your Body Type. Eating Body Type balancing foods is like getting the right gas for your car: when it's fueled properly it runs like a dream.

We're All Different

Before you start on your exciting journey into self-healing, there is something you need to understand right from the start. There are no two Air, Fire, or Earth Body Types that are exactly alike, even though they may be dominated by the same elemental-energy. Each person has a unique blend of all three elemental-energies (Air, Fire, and Earth) in their constitution. That means there are no two menus that will be exactly the same or have the same effect. Designing a daily menu that is exactly right for your Body Type is the first step toward feeling strong, vital, healthy, and balanced.

Less Means Less and More Means More

It's important to understand the "Less" and "More" that are used to suggest particular foods.

"Less" really means "don't overdo it." When you see a food that is prescribed "Less" for your Body Type, it's a signal that you can eat that particular substance in moderate amounts; not zero—you don't have to eliminate it forever. "More" really means "favor." For example, if you're eating meat, select one that has the potential to balance your Body Type over a meat that (in large quantities) may imbalance your Body Type. You'll also see * or ** in the food lists: * means "in moderation" and ** means "occasionally"; keep this in mind when choosing your foods.

The Air, Fire, and Earth Nutritional Balancing Guides are not designed to be followed obsessively. They are not "diets" to be strictly applied, they are guidelines not rules. Anything that you adhere to rigidly will create stress, and that's exactly what we're trying to avoid. Be flexible about your eating. Don't beat yourself up if you have a day or even a month of eating all "Less" foods. The beauty of the Balancing Guides is that they can be adopted anytime and anywhere, and as soon as you start back on them, they'll begin to rebalance your system and increase your GirlForce, immediately.

The key to the Balancing Guides is to be gentle with yourself. If you review the food tables for your Body Type and they look completely different from your normal eating patterns, then just apply one food at a time, slowly and gently. The experience of eating according to the Nutritional Balancing Guides should not be hard, although it would be silly to suggest that it won't take effort to change your eating patterns, especially if that requires giving up bad habits like too much junk, fast food, or too many sweets.

Eating foods that are right for your Body Type unleashes the power of GirlForce. Why? Because every time you do something healing and nurturing for yourself—like eating healthy foods—you instantly feel good. It's an empowering way to live.

In the end the best guide is your own intuition. You'll know when it's the right time to change your eating patterns, and if you listen to your instincts they will even tell you which foods will balance or imbalance you. The food suggestions presented in the Nutritional Balancing Guides will become second nature, and in time, you'll open the floodgates to new reserves of GirlForce.

Now you're ready to learn about the foods that will balance your particular Body Type and increase your GirlForce.

The Six Tastes

Ever scarfed down a burger and felt hungry twenty minutes later? One reason we feel dissatisfied after some meals is because we don't get the Six Tastes in our menus. The ancient sages of India believed that in order to feel satisfied, be healthy, and digest food properly we need a varied palette of tastes and textures. They believed that eating meals that contained the Six Tastes (Sweet, Sour, Salty, Bitter, Pungent, and Astringent) would not only give you a wholesome diet, it would also eliminate cravings.

Sweet: The sweet taste is said to nourish and comfort the body and mind and relieve hunger. All Body Types need sweet tastes in their diet, but Fire and Air Types benefit more from sweetness than Earth Types. Almost all foods contain some element of sweetness. Both water and milk are sweet, and it's the dominant taste of most foods. Bread and all the grains, many fruits, most meats, oils, most legumes, nuts, many vegetables, sugar, and honey are all sweet.

Sour: The sour taste is used in small quantities by all Body Types but is most beneficial for Air Types. Sour is also beneficial for Earth Types in small amounts and Fire Types need only a little to balance their constitutions. The sour taste helps promote digestion and speeds the elimination of wastes from the body. Many fruits, such as citrus fruits and strawberries (unless they're very sweet), are classified as sour. Fermented foods, such as miso, cheese, yogurt, sour cream, vinegar, and pickles, are also sour.

Salty: The salty taste can be used in small quantities by all Body Types but is mostly beneficial to the Air Type. It is said to cleanse the bodily tissues and activate digestion. Obviously salt is salty, but foods such as seaweed are considered salty as are anchovies and soy sauce.

Bitter: The bitter taste is beneficial for all Types. It is said to detoxify the body, cleanse the liver, tone the organs, and help purify the skin. It is most beneficial for Fire, is moderately useful for Earth, and is less important for the Air Type. Foods considered bitter are leafy green vegetables, horseradish, turmeric, aloe vera, endive, and some lettuces.

Pungent: The pungent taste is very useful for the Earth Type as it stimulates the appetite and reduces mucous. Fire Types should use this taste in moderation, as it's too stimulating. It can be beneficial to the Air Type in small amounts. Spicy foods such as Thai and Indian, which use a lot of seasonings such as onions, radishes, garlic, pepper, and ginger, are considered pungent.

Astringent: Similar to bitter. In small quantities the astringent taste is beneficial for all Types. Fire and Earth can use astringent tastes more often than Air Types. The astringent taste has a drying effect on bodily secretions (which is why it's not recommended for Air Types in large quantities). Beans and lentils, pomegranates, tea, unripe bananas, many vegetables, cabbage, broccoli, and foods that have a mouth-puckering effect are astringent.

The Air Nutritional Balancing Guide

Foods for Air Types to Favor

The Air Nutritional Balancing Guide is not a diet in the traditional sense of calorie restrictions or a prescription to eat one food group over another. It simply offers a range of food options (from all food groups) that are designed to help balance Air Types.

AIR GIRLS THRIVE WHEN THEY EAT:

Warm foods with heavy, oily textures
Sweet, sour, and salty tastes
Soothing and satisfying foods

MEAT & ANIMAL FOODS

More Beef, Chicken (dark meat), Duck eggs, Fish (freshwater or ocean), Mackerel, Salmon, Sardines, Seafood, Tuna, Turkey (dark meat)
Less Chicken (white meat), Lamb, Pork, Rabbit, Venison, Turkey (white)

FRUIT

More Most sweet fruit: Apples (cooked), Apricots, Avocados, Bananas, Berries, Cherries, Coconuts, Dates (fresh), Grapefruit, Grapes, Kiwi fruit, Lemons, Limes, Mangoes, Melons, Oranges, Papayas, Peaches, Pineapples (sweet), Plums, Prunes (soaked), Raisins (soaked), Rhubarb, Strawberries
Less Most dried fruit: Apples (raw), Pears, Persimmons, Pomegranates, Prunes (dry), Raisins (dry), Watermelons

DAIRY

More Most dairy foods: Butter, Buttermilk, Cheese (soft), Cottage cheese, Cow's milk, Ghee, Goat's cheese, Goat's milk, Ice cream,* Sour cream,* Yogurt (diluted and spiced)
Less Cheese (hard), Yogurt (plain or frozen)*

GRAINS

More Oats (cooked), Rice, Spelt, Wheat
Less Barley, Buckwheat cereals, Corn, Couscous, Granola, Millet, Muesli, Oats (dry), Pasta, Polenta, Rye, Sago, Tapioca, Wheat bran

LEGUMES

More Lentils,* Mung beans
Less Adzuki beans, Black beans, Black-eyed peas, Chick peas, Kidney beans, Lentils (brown), Lima beans, Miso,** Navy/Pinto beans, Peas (dried), Soy beans, Split peas, White beans

SEEDS

More Flaxseed, Pumpkin, Sesame, Sunflower
Less Popcorn

VEGETABLES

More Vegetables should be mostly cooked: Asparagus, Beets, Brussels sprouts (cooked), Carrots, Cucumbers, Fennel, Garlic, Green beans, Green chili peppers, Leeks, Olives (black), Onions, Parsnips, Peas, Pumpkins, Radishes* (cooked), Spinach (cooked), Squash, Sweet Potatoes, Tomatoes (cooked), Zucchini

Less Frozen, raw, and dried vegetables are to be avoided: Artichokes, Broccoli, Cabbages, (raw), Cauliflower (raw), Celery, Corn, Eggplants, Leafy greens,* Lettuce,* Mushrooms, Olives (green), Onions (raw), Parsley, Peas (raw), Peppers (sweet and hot), Potatoes (white), Sprouts, Spinach (raw), Tomatoes (raw), Turnips

NUTS

More All nuts in moderation: Almonds, Brazil nuts, Cashews, Coconuts, Hazelnuts, Macadamia nuts, Pecans, Pine nuts, Pistachios, Walnuts
Less Peanuts

BEVERAGES

More Almond milk; Aloe vera juice; Apple cider; Apricot juice; Berry juice; Carrot juice; Chai (warmed, spiced with milk); Cherry juice; Grape juice; Grapefruit juice; Herbal teas: Chamomile, Clove, Fennel, Ginger (fresh), Lemongrass, Licorice, Marshmallow, Orange peel, Peppermint, Raspberry, Rosehip, Mango juice; Miso soup; Orange juice; Peach nectar; Pineapple juice; Rice milk; Sour juices; Soy milk (warm and spiced)

Less Avoid cold drinks in general. Apple juice; Black tea; Caffeinated drinks; Carbonated drinks; Carob; Chocolate milk; Coffee; Cold dairy drinks; Cranberry juice; Herbal teas: Alfalfa, Barley, Blackberry, Dandelion, Ginseng, Hibiscus, Jasmine,** Red clover,** Red Zinger,** Sage, Strawberry; Iced tea; Mixed vegetable juices; Pear juice; Soy milk (cold); Tomato juice

HERBS & SPICES

More All spices are good:
Allspice, Almond extract, Basil,
Bay leaves, Black pepper,*
Cardamom, Cayenne,*
Cinnamon, Cloves, Coriander,*
Cumin, Dill, Fennel, Garlic,
Ginger, Marjoram, Mint, Mustard
seeds, Nutmeg, Orange peel,
Oregano, Paprika, Parsley,
Peppermint, Poppy seeds,
Rosemary, Saffron, Sage, Salt,
Spearmint, Star anise, Tarragon,
Thyme, Turmeric, Vanilla
Less Caraway

CONDIMENTS

More Chutney (sweet, spicy),
Kelp, Ketchup, Kombu, Lemon,
Lime, Mayonnaise, Mustard,
Pickles, Salt, Seaweed, Soy sauce,
Tamari, Vinegar
Less Chili peppers, Chocolate,
Horseradish

SWEETENERS

More Barley,* Malt,*
Fructose, Fruit juice
concentrates, Honey,
Molasses, Rice syrup
Less Maple syrup,**
White sugar

OILS

More Ghee, Olive, Sesame, and
most other oils
Less Flaxseed

Guidelines for Balancing Air

- Air has cold, dry qualities so warm, moist, nourishing foods such as
  stews, creamy curries, and foods like oatmeal have a beneficial effect on
  your Body Type.
- Cold, dry foods like raw vegetables, icy-cold drinks, and salads aggravate
  the Air elemental-energy.
- Sweet, soothing foods such as puddings with cream, stewed fruit, soups,
  hot cereals, warm milk, freshly baked breads are good for calming the
  sometimes nervy Air Body Type.
- Air Types are easily disturbed and have sensitive digestion. It's important
  for Air Types to create a calm, quiet atmosphere around mealtimes.
- Many Air Types experience a late afternoon energy low. A cup of hot
  tea (not coffee) and a sweet cookie will help alleviate this.

- Pungent foods are generally not attractive to Air Types; however, oily, spicy, or rich creamy foods will often satisfy an Air Type.
- While Air Types benefit from sweet tastes, sugar and sweets can give the Air Type an instant energy rush that is followed by a slump. Sugary tastes should be taken with milk or some other nourishing food like hot oatmeal.
- Sweet fruits are good for Air Types.
- Dry, salty snacks, such as chips or dry cookies, are not beneficial for Air Types. Instead, go for unsalted nuts, favoring the oily nuts such as macadamias or cashews.
- Cold, light, low-cal, low-fat, dry, and raw foods imbalance Air. If you're a salad lover, make sure you add a nourishing dressing. Sesame oil is particularly good.
- Generally, Air Types can eat large quantities of food. If you're feeling nervous, you may be tempted to eat furiously in this state. Make sure you eat moderately and try to eat as many warm foods as you can.
- To balance Air during the day, start the day with a substantial warm breakfast.
- Air Types should eat regularly and avoid any type of fasting.

Healthy Eating Habits for Air Types

By now you've probably had years of grief from your friends and family about your irregular eating habits. You love to stay up late, eat only when you feel like it, and push lettuce leaves around your plate. On the whole, Air Types are often not that interested in food, but oddly enough (sorry to say it but Mom is right) it's beneficial for you to eat at regular intervals during the day. Air Types need to eat three, even four, substantial meals a day with healthy snacks, such as nuts, in between.

When Air girls eat regularly and add warming, nourishing, and soothing foods to their menus, they'll see a marked decline in nervousness, anxiety, restlessness, depression, insomnia, and nightmares. Working with the quirks of their Body Type, not beating themselves up, and learning to enjoy the pleasures of food help Air girls accept themselves and discover balance, stamina, and vitality.

The Fire Nutritional Balancing Guide

Foods for Fire Types to Favor

The Fire Nutritional Balancing Guide is not a diet in the traditional sense of calorie restrictions or a prescription to eat one food group over another. It simply offers a range of food options (from all food groups) that are designed to help balance Fire Types.

**FIRE GIRLS
THRIVE WHEN THEY EAT:**

Cold or warm foods
Foods with moderately
heavy textures
Sweet, bitter, and astringent tastes
Not too much butter or fat

Guidelines for Balancing Fire

- The most important dietary principle for the Fire Type is to keep food cool (not icy-cold), particularly in summer.
- Fire Types generally have extremely robust digestive systems. As a result, Fire Types can take their naturally strong digestive systems for granted and eat more than they should. It's important for Fire Types not to eat too much or use too many spices or too much salt.
- The best tastes for balancing Fire are sweet, bitter, and astringent.
- Excessive fire tends to make the body sour (think smelly breath and perspiration). To prevent this, Fire Types should avoid pickles, yogurt, sour cream, and cheese.
- Processed foods, foods loaded with animal fats, fried foods, and heavily spiced foods, carbonated drinks, caffeine, alcohol, and fermented foods will all aggravate the Fire elemental-energy.
- While all Body Types can survive on a vegetarian diet, these diets are not for everyone. Fire girls should try preparing and eating lots of new and different veggies. Uncooked vegetables, cool fruit drinks, and calming herbs will keep the Fire Type balanced and healthy.

Healthy Eating Habits for Fire Types

Were you the kid who pushed everyone out of the way to get to the front of the line in the cafeteria? Fire girls are famous for their eagerness to eat (what an understatement) and get grumpy and moody when they're forced to wait for food or skip a meal.

Fire Types generally require three standard meals a day. It's important for you to keep meal times scheduled. It's also important to try not to comfort eat or eat on the run. Rashes, pimples, sour stomach, and temper flares are the result of too much fire in the body, which builds up when Fire girls are going at life a million miles an hour and stuffing food down at irregular times. Make sure you eat slowly and include cooling, soothing foods such as fresh fruits, juices, ice cream, and sweet protein such as chicken to feel calmer, happier, and more sweet-natured. Remember, it's not always cool to be hot! Fire girls need to chill with a long cool drink.

VEGETABLES

More Most sweet and bitter vegetables: Artichokes (globe), Asparagus, Beets (cooked), Broccoli, Brussels sprouts, Cabbages, Carrots (cooked), Cauliflower, Celery, Cucumbers, Fennel, Green beans, Kale, Leafy greens, Leeks (cooked), Lettuce, Mushrooms, Okra, Olives (black), Onions (cooked), Parsnips, Peas, Peppers (sweet), Potatoes, Pumpkins, Radishes (cooked), Spinach (cooked), Sprouts, Squash, Taro root, Wheatgrass, Zucchini

Less Avoid pungent vegetables: Beet greens, Beets (raw), Carrots (raw), Corn, Eggplants, Garlic, Green chilies, Horseradish, Leeks (raw), Mustard greens, Olives (green), Onions (raw), Peppers (hot), Radishes (raw), Spinach (raw), Tomatoes, Turnips, Watercress

LEGUMES

More Adzuki beans, Black beans, Black-eyed peas, Chick peas, Kidney beans, Lentils (brown and red), Lima beans, Mung beans, Navy/Pinto beans, Peas (dried), Soy beans, Tofu, White beans

Less Green lentils

SEEDS

More Flaxseed, Popcorn (buttered, no salt), Psyllium, Pumpkin, Sunflower

Less Sesame

NUTS

More Almonds (soaked and peeled), Coconuts

Less Almonds (with skin), Brazil nuts, Cashews, Hazelnuts, Macadamia nuts, Peanuts, Pecans, Pine nuts, Pistachios, Walnuts

GRAINS

More Barley cereal (dry), Couscous, Granola, Oat bran, Oats (cooked), Pasta, Rice (basmati, white, wild), Sago, Spelt, Wheat

Less Bread (with yeast), Corn, Millet, Muesli, Oats (dry), Polenta, Rice (brown), Rye

FRUIT

More Most sweet fruits: Apples, Apricots, Avocados, Berries (sweet), Cherries, Coconuts, Dates, Figs, Grapes (dark), Mangoes, Melons, Oranges, Pears, Pineapples (sweet), Pomegranates, Prunes, Raisins, Watermelons

Less Avoid sour fruit: Bananas, Cranberries, Grapefruit, Grapes (Green), Kiwi fruit,** Lemons, Limes,** Mangoes (green), Papayas,** Peaches, Persimmons, Rhubarb, Strawberries

BEVERAGES

More Almond milk; Aloe vera juice; Apple juice; Apricot juice; Berry juice; Black tea; Chai (warm and sweet with milk); Cherry juice; Cool dairy drinks; Grape juice; Herbal teas: Alfalfa, Barley, Blackberry, Chamomile, Dandelion, Elderflower, Fennel, Ginger (fresh), Hibiscus, Jasmine, Lemon balm, Orange peel, Peppermint, Raspberry, Red clover, Spearmint; Mango juice; Mixed vegetable juice; Peach nectar; Pear juice; Prune juice; Rice milk; Soy milk

Less Apple cider; Caffeinated drinks; Carbonated drinks; Carrot juice; Chocolate milk; Coffee; Cranberry juice; Herbal teas: Basil, Cinnamon, Clove, Ginger (dried), Ginseng, Red Zinger, Rosehip, Sage; Iced tea; Icy-cold drinks; Lemonade; Miso soup; Pineapple juice; Sour juices; Tomato juice; V-8 juice

MEAT & ANIMAL FOODS

More Chicken (white meat), Eggs (whites/albumen only), Fish (freshwater), Rabbit, Turkey (white meat), Venison

Less Beef, Chicken (dark meat), Fish (ocean), Lamb, Pork, Salmon, Sardines, Seafood, Tuna, Turkey (dark meat)

SWEETENERS

More Barley malt, Fructose, Fruit juice concentrates, Maple syrup, Rice syrup

Less Honey, Molasses

DAIRY

More Butter (unsalted), Cheese (soft, unsalted), Cottage cheese, Cow's milk, Goat's milk, Goat's cheese, Ice cream

Less Butter (salted), Buttermilk Cheese (hard and aged), Sour cream, Yogurt (frozen or with fruit)

HERBS & SPICES

More Basil, Black pepper,* Cardamom,* Cinnamon, Coriander, Cumin, Dill, Fennel, Garlic, Ginger (fresh), Mint, Orange peel,* Parsley,* Peppermint, Saffron, Spearmint, Turmeric, Vanilla

Less Allspice, Almond extract, Basil, Bay leaves, Cayenne, Cloves, Garlic, Ginger (dried), Marjoram, Mustard seeds, Nutmeg, Oregano, Paprika, Parsley, Poppy seeds, Rosemary, Sage, Salt, Tarragon, Thyme

CONDIMENTS

More Chutney (sweet)

Less Chocolate, Chutney (spicy), Horseradish, Kelp, Ketchup, Kombu,** Lemon, Mayonnaise, Mustard, Pickles, Salt (in excess), Seaweed, Soy sauce, Tamari,* Vinegar

OILS

More Canola, Flaxseed, Ghee, Olive, Soybean, Sunflower, Walnut

Less Almond, Corn, Safflower, Sesame

The Earth Nutritional Balancing Guide

Foods for Earth Types to Favor

The Earth Nutritional Balancing Guide is not a diet in the traditional sense of calorie restrictions or a prescription to eat one food group over another. It simply offers a range of food options (from all food groups) that are designed to help balance Earth Types.

EARTH GIRLS THRIVE WHEN THEY EAT:

Warm, light foods
Dry foods cooked without much water
Minimal butter and fats
Pungent and astringent tastes
Stimulating, spicy foods

Guidelines for Balancing Earth

- Overeating is the Achilles' heel of the Earth Type. The best Earth balancing foods are light, dry, and warm, and have mostly spicy, bitter, and astringent tastes. In fact, bitter and astringent tastes help curb the Earth Type's appetite.
- Eat small meals, especially if they are made up of low-fat foods, lightly cooked vegetables, and sour fruits.
- Spices such as ginger, turmeric, pepper, garlic, cinnamon, and paprika help stimulate the Earth Type's slow digestive system.
- Avoid cold, sweet, and heavy tastes and textures; for example, ice cream is not a balancing food for Earth.
- Select hot over cold at every meal.
- Don't skip meals, particularly breakfast, which provides a nourishing start to the day.
- Avoid fried foods.
- Go for salads, fresh fruit, and fiber.
- Combat early morning lethargy by drinking a glass of warm water with lemon and ginger.

FRUIT
More Most astringent fruits:
Apples, Apricots, Berries, Cherries,
Cranberries, Figs (dried), Lemons,
Limes, Peaches, Pears,
Persimmons, Pomegranates,
Prunes, Raisins, Strawberries
Less Sweet and sour fruits:
Avocados, Bananas, Coconuts,
Dates, Figs (fresh), Grapes,**
Grapefruit, Kiwi fruit, Mangoes,
Melons, Oranges, Papaya,
Pineapple, Plums, Rhubarb,
Watermelons

DAIRY
More Butter* (unsalted), Goat's cheese,
Yogurt (plain, skimmed milk)
Less Butter (salted), Buttermilk, Cheese,
Cow's milk, Ice cream, Sour cream,
Yogurt (frozen or with fruit)

OILS
More Almond, Canola, Corn,
Olive,* Sunflower
Less Avocado, Coconut,
Safflower, Sesame, Soy, Walnut

NUTS

More Dry nuts such as Almonds, Hazelnuts, Walnuts

Less Oily nuts such as Brazil nuts, Cashews, Macadamias, Peanuts

SEEDS

More Flaxseed,* Popcorn (no butter or salt), Pumpkin,* Sunflower,*

Less Psyllium,** Sesame

BEVERAGES

More Apple cider; Apple juice*; Apricot juice; Berry juice; Black tea (spiced); Carob; Carrot juice; Cherry juice; Cranberry juice; Fresh vegetable juice; Grain "coffee"; Grape juice; Herbal teas: Alfalfa, Barley, Blackberry, Chamomile, Cinnamon, Clove, Dandelion, Fennel, Ginger (fresh), Ginseng, Hibiscus, Jasmine, Lemon, Orange peel, Peppermint, Raspberry, Red clover, Spearmint; Mango juice; Peach nectar; Pear juice; Prune juice; Soy milk (hot and spicy)

Less Caffeinated drinks; Carbonated drinks; Chocolate milk; Coffee; Herbal teas: Basil, Clove, Ginger (dried), Red Zinger, Rosehip, Sage; Iced tea; Icy-cold drinks; Lemonade; Miso soup; Orange juice; Pineapple juice; Sour juices; Tomato juice; V-8 juice

GRAINS

More Barley, Buckwheat, Cereal (cold, dry, or puffed), Corn, Couscous, Granola, Millet, Muesli, Oat bran, Oats (dry), Polenta, Rice (basmati, wild), Rye, Sago, Tapioca, Wheat bran

Less Bread (with yeast), Hot cereals and steamed grains, Oats (cooked), Pasta, Rice (brown, white), Wheat

HERBS & SPICES

More All spices are good: Allspice, Almond extract, Basil, Bay leaf, Black pepper, Cardamom, Cayenne, Cinnamon, Cloves, Coriander, Cumin, Dill, Fennel,* Garlic, Ginger (fresh), Marjoram, Mint, Mustard seeds, Nutmeg, Orange peel, Oregano, Paprika, Parsley, Peppermint, Poppy seeds, Rosemary, Saffron, Sage, Spearmint, Tarragon, Thyme, Turmeric, Vanilla*

Less Salt

MEAT & ANIMAL FOODS

More Chicken (white meat), Eggs, Fish (freshwater), Rabbit, Shrimp, Turkey (white meat)

Less Beef, Chicken (dark meat), Duck, Fish (ocean), Lamb, Pork, Salmon, Sardines, Tuna, Turkey (dark meat)

VEGETABLES

More Most bitter and pungent vegetables: Artichoke (globe), Asparagus, Beet greens, Beets, Broccoli, Brussels sprouts, Cabbages, Carrots, Cauliflower, Celery, Corn, Eggplants, Fennel, Green beans, Green chilies, Horseradish, Kale, Leafy greens, Leeks, Lettuce, Mushrooms, Mustard greens, Okra, Onions, Parsley, Peas, Peppers (sweet and hot), Potatoes, Radishes, Spinach, Sprouts, Squash, Tomatoes (cooked), Turnips, Watercress, Wheatgrass

Less Avoid sweet and juicy vegetables: Cucumbers, Olives (black and green), Parsnips,** Pumpkin, Squash, Sweet potatoes, Taro root, Tomatoes (raw), Zucchini

LEGUMES

More Adzuki beans, Black beans, Black-eyed peas, Chick peas, Lentils (brown and red), Lima beans, Navy/Pinto beans, Peas (dried), Soy beans, White beans
Less Kidney beans, Mung beans

CONDIMENTS
More Chili peppers, Chutney (spicy), Horseradish, Mustard (without vinegar)
Less Chocolate, Chutney (sweet), Kelp, Ketchup,** Mayonnaise, Pickles, Salt, Seaweed,** Soy sauce, Tamari, Vinegar

SWEETENERS
More Fruit juice concentrates, Honey (raw not processed)
Less Barley malt, Fructose, Maple syrup, Molasses, Palm sugar, Rice syrup, White sugar

Healthy Eating Habits for Earth Types

Of all the Body Types, you are the one that is most likely to be carrying a little extra weight. You may not be overweight, but you've probably noticed that you're curvier than the skinny minis in your class. In a society that focuses on thin girls, it's not always easy being a voluptuous Earth babe. Fear not, eating for your Body Type will help you maintain good health and a robust self-esteem.

Earth gals tend not to feel ravenous, even though you enjoy your food and can be quite solidly built. You're often not terribly hungry in the mornings, and it's perfectly okay for you to have a light breakfast of fruit and yogurt; you'll feel lighter and less sluggish. Earth Types have slow digestive systems and may find that it takes up to six hours to digest the last meal. Earth Types can lean toward chubbiness, so it's vital to learn when enough is enough. Try not to fill your stomach to the limit.

In a culture that promotes only one shape and size—that is, skinny and small—girls with hips, butts, and boobs can feel alienated and unattractive. It's time to take a leaf out of Jennifer Hudson's book and get right into your yummy, curvy, sticky-outy bits and celebrate them. When Earth girls eat according to their Body Type they look healthy, strong, and radiant— the key to a positive vibe with a body to match.

Help! I'm Overweight

All of us can put on weight, especially if we eat too much junk food and do too little exercise. Sometimes weight gain is the result of a hormonal imbalance, a genetic disorder, or some other disease. If you are very overweight for your height and build, the best idea is to go and see your family doctor and talk to him or her about your issues. It's also good to remember that when we're stressed, and this goes for all Body Types, we can put on extra weight. On the whole, most people find when they eat right for their Body Type their weight stabilizes and they feel healthy and vital.

Help! I'm Underweight

There are times when stress gets the better of us, and it's easy to skip meals and eat on the run. Losing a little fat can sometimes be a good thing. Extreme weight loss is not especially healthy. If you've noticed that you've shed a lot of weight, the best idea is to see your family doctor. Eating disorders such as anorexia and bulimia are quite common among teen girls (you may have even noticed that some of your girlfriends starve themselves or throw up). Eating disorders are diseases and should be treated by a doctor. If you're rail-thin and concerned about it, make a time to see your doctor or visit a nutritionist to check that everything is cool with your body and mind.

Eat Right Hints for Every Body

Eating right for your Body Type is a total buzz. When you know you're guzzling good drinks and chowing down on yummy, healthy foods, you feel great. These hints benefit all shapes and sizes, every race and color, and certainly all Body Types:

- Eat when you're hungry.
- Do not eat when you're nervous or upset as it causes imbalances in your digestion.
- Eat fresh organic produce whenever you can.
- Eat no fewer than six servings of fresh fruits and vegetables per day.
- Include two daily servings of nuts, seeds, and legumes in your diet.
- Add lean meats, eggs, and fish to your diet. Two servings of lean meat, three servings of fish, and three or four eggs a week are safe serving suggestions.
- Eat fats, but make sure they are "good fats" such as olive oil, flaxseed oil, avocados, or nuts. Avoid manufactured fats, such as margarine; refined oils, such as canola oil; and the refined fats that are in processed cookies, chips, frozen pies, and pastries.
- Avoid processed foods, fast foods, and fried foods.
- Avoid unripe fruits and vegetables.
- Try not to eat leftovers. Microwaved food and reheated food have little energy.
- Eat with friends or loved ones.
- Once in a while eat in complete silence so you can appreciate your food and its tastes.
- Give thanks for the food on your table. Gratitude actually adds energy to your food.
- Don't overfill your stomach.
- Avoid icy-cold drinks and carbonated drinks before, during, and after a meal. Instead, sip room temperature water with your meal.
- Don't watch television while you eat; it disturbs digestion.
- Never force yourself to eat a food you don't like.
- Chew your food until it's thoroughly soft.

- A double handful (of your own hands) of food is an ideal meal size.
- Allow your intuition to guide you about the foods and tastes that suit you.
- Try to eat regularly and at the same times each day.
- Eat foods that are produced locally and are in season. For example, eating watermelon (which has its peak season in summer) in the middle of winter is not great for any Body Type.
- Wait an hour after eating before doing any strenuous exercise.
- Don't meditate on a full stomach.
- Don't go to bed on a full stomach.

- Avoid rich food and dairy food in the evening.
- Eat food that has been prepared with loving hands—it contains more energy.
- Drink at least one quart of water daily.
- One idea is to pin a copy of the food lists to your refrigerator so that you can select foods from the fridge or pantry according to your Body Type. It means that snacking, which can be a fairly unconscious act, is transformed into a conscious dietary practice.

Eating right for your Body Type is a mega **confidence booster**. The simple fact that you know you're doing **something good**, healthy, nurturing, and **kind for yourself** gives you a warm glow—that feeling, the **inner power** you get from looking after yourself is **GirlForce**.

Get Munching, Girl

Starving yourself is not cool or healthy. Overeating as a way to beat the blues isn't too smart either. Listen to your body, tune into the foods that balance your Body Type, and get with the GirlForce game.

Now that you've had a chance to look at your Body Type food suggestions, you'll probably find there are a lot of foods that you already like and eat regularly. The next step is to design your meals based on the foods you enjoy and work them into your daily life.

If you've been stalking diners, ice cream shops, and fast food joints, it's going to feel weird to start adding heaps of fresh fruit and veggies and healthy snacks. The best thing to do is go to your local health food store and start trying, one by one, the healthy foods on offer. Taking bags of nuts, seeds, and dried fruits to school every day is one way to start healthy snacking. Another way is to make up a pot of soup once a week, loaded up with Body Type balancing veggies, beans, and grains, and slurp on it every time you're hungry.

Enlist the help of your mom or dad; ask them if they can pick up Body Type balancing foods for you next time they do the shopping. If you provide them with a list of things and stock the fridge and pantry with the right kinds of foods, you'll find you'll begin to snack regularly on healthy things and effortlessly eat less of the things that are not balancing for your Body Type.

It's also much more fun, and you'll discover more about the cool art and science of eating right for your Body Type, if you discuss it with your friends. You'll get insights into your tastes and desires, and you'll swap helpful hints and ideas when you talk about the quirks and qualities of your particular Body Type. Share the secrets, pass on the fun tips and techniques. It's awesome when you share the info!

NO PAIN, NO GAIN?
NO THANKS! HERE'S
HOW TO DESIGN A
HEALTHY STRESS-FREE
ROUTINE FOR YOUR
BODY TYPE THAT'S JAM-
PACKED WITH HIGH-
INTENSITY BURSTS TO
KICK-START YOUR
ENERGY, PLUS YOGA
MOVES TO HELP YOU
CHILL OUT. IT'S THE
PERFECT COMBO TO
GET YOU INTO THE
GIRLFORCE GROOVE.

CHAPTER FOUR

DIY Body Blast

Some **chicks** thrive on go-for-the-burn style **exercise** while others benefit from gentle, **low-impact sports**. Discover what kind of exercise will **balance** your **Body Type** and give you enough **oomph** and get-up-and-go to boost your **GirlForce**.

EVER BEEN IN ONE OF THOSE GYM CLASSES where your phys ed teacher
made the whole class run around the track ten times? If we look at the
gym class from the point of view of Body Types, the chances are that the
Fire chicks were the ones who ran hard and competitively and were
determined to win; the Air girls were probably the ones who tired
quickly and struggled with the distance and the discipline needed to get
to the end; and the Earth babes were most likely the slow and steady
ones who protested about the effort required to make the distance (not
lovin' rigorous exercise) but reached the finish line without burning out.

The reason not everyone in the class made the ten laps like a pro
is that when it comes to exercise we not only have different fitness levels,
we also have different Body Types and different needs and desires.

The Western approach to exercise, which has been set in stone for
decades, has been based on the principle "what's good for one is good
for all." The GirlForce philosophy offers a completely different view.
Instead, I say:

You're an individual,
and only a program
that is specially
tailored to your
needs will balance
your Body Type and
boost your GirlForce.

Air

Exercise Guidelines for Air Types

The agile and fast Air girl is designed for light exercise. Heavy-duty contact sports that require stamina and a competitive spirit are not beneficial for Air Types, who get their energy in short, sharp bursts. Long distance running, for example, will tire an Air girl and deplete her GirlForce. Light aerobic exercise that involves balance, poise, and flexibility will generally suit the Air princess (it's no accident that most professional ballerinas and gymnasts are Air girls). Because Air girls are easily excited, they often take up new sports only to drop them weeks later. The Air Type must make sure that she works out for short periods and exercises out of the wind (which aggravates her energy). In winter especially, Air chicks should exercise indoors in heated rooms. Exhaustion is the Air girl's enemy, so Air Types have to make sure they don't overdo it when exercising. Nature, trees, and beachside strolls are nourishing for the Air elemental-energy. So take it easy, honey, there's no need for speed.

Recommended Exercises: Air Types naturally excel at fast-paced sports that require flexibility, agility, and sprints. The exercises that balance Air energies are generally calming and slow, such as yoga, Tai Chi, weight training, walking and light hiking, swimming (slowly on warm days), and archery.

How Long: Half an hour a day is ample for Air Types.

Where: Indoors, away from the elements, or on warm, windless mornings or afternoons in nature.

Exercise Guidelines for Fire Types

Fiery divas love a challenge. They also need to learn how to put the brakes on; they can lose their breath and become overheated, especially if they exercise in the midday sun. Fun-loving Fire gals are naturally attracted to competitive team sports where they can measure their achievements. No one benefits more from a cooling dip in a pool or a splash in the ocean than a Fire vixen. Being hot constitutionally, Fire girls make perfect mermaids. Because Fire Types are often working toward deadlines and thrive on success, they benefit enormously from the relaxation of a leisurely stroll where they can let go of the demands of work and play. The key for the Fire girl is to simply exercise without an end goal—you don't need to swim a thousand laps or run a million miles to benefit your body. You can get the adrenaline rush you love from a relaxed, fun activity rather than a killer marathon.

Recommended Exercises: Fire Types will be drawn to sports that call on their natural athletic ability, speed, and mental discipline. They benefit from noncompetitive sports that offer the possibility of pure enjoyment rather than winning, such as yoga, hiking, jogging, swimming, indoor climbing, volleyball, surfing, bodysurfing, recreational skiing, martial arts, cycling, and sailing.

How Long: Half an hour to an hour each day.

Where: Anywhere out of the midday sun.

Fire

Exercise Guidelines for Earth Types

Earth girls have real staying power. They have both stamina and athletic ability. The Earth body is generally fuller and curvier than the other Types, and as a result it is often not very agile or flexible. Earth Types benefit from hard, sustained endurance-style exercise. Earth babes often loathe exercise (sorry to bust the secret). While all Body Types benefit from regular aerobic exercise, Earth girls—who often resist this style of exercise—benefit hugely from a cardio workout. Once the Earth girl is up off the couch and at 'em, she usually finds the physical stimulation of a good workout is a real energy boost. While go-for-the-burn exercise is not good for other Types, Earth girls benefit from high-impact sports that make you sweat. Baby, you're primed for some hard-core workouts. Once you shake your booty into action, you'll feel great.

Recommended Exercises: Earth Types have natural stamina and strength. And because of their warm, inclusive natures, they enjoy team sports. The best way to balance Earth energies is to increase stimulating and vigorous activities such as: yoga, aerobics, basketball, volleyball, cycling, dance, cross-country skiing, running, soccer, tennis, squash, softball, baseball, weight training, and circuit training.

How Long: Aim for up to an hour each day.

Where: Like Air Types who feel the cold, Earth Types should make sure they stay out of cold, damp weather.

Earth

How Much Exercise Do I Need?

Why do we find it so hard to motivate ourselves to exercise?

Sure, it's easier to veg out in front of the TV than to get up and go for a walk. But in most cases, it's not the physical effort that holds us back from exercise. It's the fact that we're not exercising right for our Body Type that dampens the rush that exercise can give us.

Your Body Type can give you lots of clues to the sorts of exercise that will make you feel good about yourself and put a zing in your step. By exercising in a way that's in tune with your nature, your likes and dislikes, your strengths and weaknesses, you will discover a new way to exercise that's energizing and full-throttle fun.

Want a total confidence boost? Exercise is a form of self-love. Getting up off your butt and doing something positive and cool, like exercising, is a way of nurturing and celebrating yourself.

In pure Ayurvedic terms, Air Types should exercise lightly, Fire Types moderately, and Earth Types vigorously. In Western terms, regardless of Body Type, girls should get at least 30 minutes of moderate to intense physical activity on all or most days to reap health rewards. (And to be considered healthy it must be something that increases your cardiovascular fitness, such as a brisk walk!) If you want to go with the Ayurvedic way, the system says no matter what your Body Type is, you need to go at your own pace as you build your fitness and get into the exercise groove. If you follow the guidelines for your Body Type, you'll find you'll do away with the need for complicated routines and assessments. And the idea that you can forget about calculating whether you're "fat-burning" or whether you're "doing enough" is incredibly empowering. One final word: before you begin any exercise program seek advice from your doctor or a professional coach.

Get up to speed with exercise and make sure it:

Is Right for You

There is no single exercise program that will benefit everyone. Unless we do the right amount of exercise to keep our heart, muscles, lungs, bones, and joints healthy, we will do little to boost GirlForce and maintain our well-being. Discovering the kinds of activities that act as "medicines" for our bodies and souls opens up a new pathway to healing.

Will Boost GirlForce

Even though the health benefits of exercise are indisputable, people struggle to find the motivation to do it regularly. One reason we lack motivation is that society has focused principally on the physical rewards that exercise can deliver (tight butt, thin arms, toned abs) and has ignored the emotional and spiritual benefits of exercise.

The concept that my GirlForce philosophy promotes is that exercise must be a GirlForce-enhancing practice. And it can only be a GirlForce-enhancing practice if it's joyous, creative, spiritually and emotionally uplifting, challenging, and enjoyable. Exercise is a form of meditation, a time when we can switch off from the hassles of life and tune in to our vital and ecstatic spiritual selves. Using exercise as a spiritual channel is one of the most powerful and satisfying ways to experience the bliss of existence.

Is Great Fun

The Western idea of "no pain, no gain" is completely contrary to the GirlForce philosophy! Pain is nature's way of alerting us to a problem. Pain in exercise is a sign that we have gone too far, our muscles are burning, our tendons and ligaments are overstretching, and our hearts are straining. Forcing ourselves to exercise causes stress, and stress is one of the main drains on our GirlForce. When we enjoy exercise our hearts, muscles, blood, and lymph and immune systems enjoy it too. Freed from the "one-size-fits-all" philosophies, you'll find exercise can be a great way to discover your unique body and mind.

Fits into Your Busy Schedule

The experts tell us we need at least 30 minutes of exercise at least five times a week to maintain our health and well-being. It's possible to get the same benefits out of three 10-minute sessions, which function as a complete 30-minute program. Which means that you can ditch the idea of a strict regime like going to the gym at a set time. Instead, you can get fit by dancing around the house with your hairbrush, playing soccer in the park with your friends, or walking to school instead of taking the bus. Or, you can set aside a time every day, "your time" to exercise—some girls find they need to schedule the 150 minutes per week into their calendar. Others find that 10 minutes of yoga in the morning and an evening stroll around the block with their friend does the trick. The key is to discover ways to slip exercise into your life. Exercise needs to become as natural as brushing your teeth or going to sleep—easy and effortless.

Yoga for Your Body Type

Yoga—so what's it all about? Here, you'll discover everything you always wanted to know about this ancient practice but were too shy to ask.

Given all the hype (every celebrity on the planet seems to swear by it), you could be forgiven for thinking that yoga is a hot new fitness fad. The truth is it goes way back, before the current fashion-fest, to India and the 5,000-year-old wisdom of Ayurveda.

Yoga literally means "union." Practitioners believe that when we balance and unify the mind, body, and spirit we feel powerful, contented, energized, and strong. Yoga in its pure form is a path to enlightenment. And at this level, it's a spiritual practice in its own right. Yoga can also function simply and effectively as a therapeutic physical practice that can deliver a lot of benefits when done regularly.

If there is one exercise that can bestow universal benefits, it is yoga. Yoga is medicine to all Body Types. No matter what other exercise options you choose, if you include a little Body Type balancing yoga in your daily routine you'll notice health rewards in next to no time. You don't need to shave your head or join a cult to perform yoga. All you need is a few minutes a day and the courage to make like a pretzel.

yoga for your body type

air fire earth

The combination of Body Type-specific yoga and some fun, high-intensity workouts such as soccer, boxing, running, or basketball form the perfect exercise pattern. Throw yourself into exercise. Get out there every day and go for it.

Are You a Poser?

Yoga postures or "asanas" are specific body positions that stretch and strengthen the muscles, joints, ligaments, and tissues. According to the ancient yogic scriptures, there were originally 8,400,000 postures, but over the centuries the yogic masters modified and reduced the number of postures to the few hundred we know today.

Here you will learn only a handful of yoga postures, but the regular practice of those postures will help stimulate your nervous system, improve concentration, remove muscle aches and pains, boost circulation, and increase GirlForce. The ancient sages of India indicated that there were certain postures that were suitable for particular Body Types.

There is no right and wrong in yoga. Everybody is different. The most important part of doing yoga is to work to your own level and never force your body beyond its limits. *Yoga teaches us to accept ourselves and our bodies.*

Some postures may be too hard in the beginning. In fact, there will always be some postures that are difficult and some that are easy. Don't push yourself to hang in a posture if it hurts!

The more you practice yoga, the more you will notice your body changing, becoming stronger and more flexible. The joy comes from the exploration of your unique body and mind.

For a complete health-promoting routine, you only need a series of five postures that are right for your Body Type. These balanced moves will help maximize your flexibility and stamina and at the same time will calm the mind and soothe the spirit.

AIR TYPE POSTURES

The Air routine can be performed for 15 to 30 minutes.
The movements should be slow, gentle, smooth, and restful.

Air

1. Palm Tree Pose

Instructions

Stand with your feet slightly apart and your arms by your sides. Distribute the weight of your body evenly over both feet.

Interlock your fingers and push your palms toward the floor. Slowly raise your arms above your head, keeping the arms straight. Place your hands on top of your head. Fix your eyes on a point slightly above the level of your head. Your eyes should remain fixed on this point throughout the practice.

Inhale and stretch your arms, shoulders, and chest upward.

Raise your heels and come up onto your toes. Stretch your whole body from the top to the bottom without losing balance or moving your feet.

Hold the breath and the position for a few seconds. Then lower your heels while breathing out and bring your hands back to the top of your head.

Relax for a few seconds before performing the next round.

Do this 5 to 10 times.

Benefits: This basic standing pose helps strengthen the legs and develops physical and mental balance. The whole of the spine is stretched and loosened, which helps stimulate the nerves along the spinal column.

2. Cat Pose

Instructions

Kneel on the floor with your hands directly under the shoulders. Your knees should be directly under your hips, an inch or two apart, and the spine parallel to the floor. (Basically you should look like a cat in its four-footed "standing" position.)

Breathing out, suck your belly button up into your spine and drop your head toward the floor. Your lower and upper back should round into an arch.

Inhale, pushing your belly button toward the floor: your tailbone will point upward. Lift your head from the dropped position and stretch your neck and head forward, opening your chest. Your upper back will arch downward stretching the lower back toward the floor.

Do both up and down arches 5 times.

Benefits: The pelvic movement in this pose increases the mobility of the hips and lower back.

3. Crocodile Pose

Instructions

Lie on your stomach and put your elbows on the floor, resting your chin in your palms. You will feel the stretch in your neck and lower back. Adjust your elbows if you do not feel the stretch or if it's too intense. Breathe naturally and rhythmically.

Hold this pose for 2 to 4 minutes.

Benefits: This posture is great for any back pain or disorder. It releases compression on the spinal nerves and also stimulates the lungs. It tones the central nervous system.

4. Cross-Legged Pose or Easy Pose with Twist

Instructions

Sit in a cross-legged position.

Inhale and place your left hand on the right knee. Reach behind your torso and put the right hand on the left thigh.

Breathe in as you lift your spine and twist the upper body toward the right and look over your right shoulder. Imagine your spine pushing through the top of your head.

Exhale, return to the front, and release your hands from where they are.

Breathe in again, reverse the hand positions, and twist in the opposite direction.

Hold the pose for 5 breaths, 5 times each side.

Benefits: This gentle twist helps tone the spine, reducing stiffness in the lower back.

5. Corpse Pose

You can practice this pose in between postures, or you can use it to finish your yoga routine. No less than 5 minutes is optimum, but take as long as you like.

Instructions

Lie flat on your back with the palms of your hands facing upward and about 6 inches away from your body.

Close your eyes and move your feet slightly apart. Make sure the head does not fall one way or the other. Become aware of the natural rhythm of the breath and allow your body to become relaxed. Begin to count the breaths from the number 27 backward to zero. If your mind wanders, bring it back to the counting.

Benefits: This posture relaxes the body and mind. It is a good practice to do before sleep or after any dynamic exercise. The more you can relax into this pose, the more you will establish "restfulness" in your body and being.

FIRE TYPE POSTURES

The Fire routine can be performed over 20 to 30 minutes.
The movements should be rigorous but not excessively fast.

Fire

1. Swaying Palm Tree Pose

Instructions

Stand with your feet about a foot and a half apart and your arms by your sides. Distribute the weight of your body evenly over both feet. Fix your gaze on a point directly in front of you.

Interlock your fingers and turn the palms outward. Breathing in, raise your arms above your head, stretching the whole body upward while keeping your feet firmly on the floor.

Bend sideways from the waist to the left, breathing out. Don't bend forward or backward, just to the side without any twisting.

Hold this position for a moment before breathing in and coming back up to the center position.

Breathe out while bringing your arms down to your sides.

Relax for a few seconds before performing the next round.

One round is moving to the left, then to the right, and releasing your arms down. Complete 5 to 10 rounds.

Benefits: The whole of the spine is stretched and loosened, which helps stimulate the nerves along the spinal column. This posture stretches and works the sides of the waist, balancing postural muscles on both sides of your body. The posture also tones the butt muscles and the intestines.

2. Swinging While Standing Pose

Instructions

Stand with your feet about 3 feet apart. Raise your arms above your head as you breathe in. Keep the elbows straight while letting your hands hang limp at the wrist.

Bend forward and swing your upper body down from your hips all the way forward so your hands and head swing through your legs—or as far as you can go. As you do this, forcefully and completely push your breath out. Making a "HA" sound helps.

Breathe in a little and swing back upward, raising your upper body so that it's parallel to the floor.

Collapse forward again, forcing out your breath and letting your hands swing between your legs a little further than last time.

Repeat this half-collapse 5 times before breathing in fully and swinging back up into the standing position, arms raised above your head.

Breathe out, lowering your arms back to your sides.

You can do this up to 5 times.

Benefits: If you weren't awake before this posture, you will be after! It stimulates the circulation, helps remove tiredness, and tones the spinal nerves. The hamstrings and back muscles get a stretch, the hips loosen, and the internal organs get a massage.

3. Half Locust Pose

Instructions

Lie flat on your stomach and place your hands under your thighs with palms facing downward or clenched.

Place your chin on the floor, slightly stretched forward. You should breathe in while in this position.

Keep both legs straight and, using your back muscles, raise your left leg off the ground as high as you can while the right leg and both hips remain in contact with the floor.

Hold the position for as long as is comfortable and then lower the leg to the floor, breathing out.

Repeat with the right leg. This is one round.

You can do up to 5 rounds vigorously or 3 rounds slowly.

Benefits: Strengthens the thighs, buttocks, and lower back muscles, helps to relieve lower back pain. It can help alleviate constipation.

4. Head to Knee Pose

Instructions

Sit on the floor with both legs stretched out in front of you.

Bend your left leg out to the side, tucking the heel of the foot up into your groin. The side of your foot should be resting on the floor with the sole of the foot against the inside of your right thigh. Your left leg will now be bent and poking out on the floor to the left of your body.

Inhale and, breathing out, slowly bend forward, sliding your hands down the right leg, bringing your upper body forward and over the straight leg.

If possible, take hold of your right foot, but only go as far as is comfortable. Hold the position for as long as you can and breathe normally. Focus on breathing into and out of the muscles you feel stretching.

Return to the starting position, breathing in.

Repeat with the right leg bent and the left leg straight. This is one round.

You can do this for up to 5 rounds.

Benefits: This posture stretches the hamstrings and increases flexibility in the hip joints. The entire abdominal and pelvic region gets a workout, along with the circulation to the nerves and muscles of the spine. It's also a fantastic posture to help you prepare to sit cross-legged for meditation.

5. Corpse Pose

You can practice this pose in between postures, or you can use it to finish your yoga routine. No less than 5 minutes is optimum, but take as long as you like.

Instructions

Lie flat on your back with the palms of your hands facing upward and about 6 inches away from your body.

Close your eyes and move your feet slightly apart. Make sure the head does not fall one way or the other. Become aware of the natural rhythm of the breath and allow your body to become relaxed. Begin to count the breaths from the number 27 backward to zero. If your mind wanders, bring it back to the counting.

Benefits: This posture relaxes the body and mind. It is good to do before sleep or after any dynamic exercise. The more you can relax into this pose the more you will establish "restfulness" in your body and being.

EARTH TYPE POSTURES

The Earth routine can be performed over 30 to 40 minutes.
The movements should be dynamic and stimulating.

Earth

1. Chopping Wood Pose

Instructions

Squat with your heels on the ground, knees spread far enough apart to allow you to bring your straightened arms inside your knees.

Clasp your hands together and rest them on the ground. Your arms should remain straight and the hands clasped throughout this exercise.

Look straight ahead. Breathe in deeply and stand up, raising your straight arms above, and if you can, behind your head, stretching the spine upward.

In one strong movement, like chopping a piece of wood, bring your arms toward the ground rapidly while squatting back into your starting position. During this movement you should force all your breath out, make a "HA" sound. This is one round.

"Chop wood" for 5 to 10 rounds.

Benefits: This pose strengthens the thighs and upper back and works difficult-to-exercise muscles between the shoulder blades, as well as the shoulder joints. It gets your energy moving in a big way.

2. Churning the Mill Pose

Instructions

Sit with your legs stretched out in front of you.

Interlock the fingers of both hands and hold your arms out in front of your chest. Your arms should remain straight and horizontal throughout the practice.

Bend forward as far as you can and imagine you're going to churn the mill—or a more up-to-date image would be that you're holding a long pen between your hands and you're going to draw as big a circle on the ground as possible. Breathe out.

Keeping your arms straight and horizontal, begin drawing this circle in a clockwise direction, first passing over your right leg, and then leaning back as far as it's possible, breathing in, and continuing the circle over your lap and so on and back to where you began. This is one round.

Do 10 rounds clockwise, then 10 rounds counterclockwise.

Benefits: This is a great posture for toning the nerves and organs of the pelvis and abdomen. It also helps to regulate your hormones.

3. Cobra Pose

Instructions

Lie flat on your stomach, arms down by your sides. Rest your chin on the floor.

Bend your elbows and place your palms on the floor beside your chest. Make sure your fingers point forward.

Slowly lift your upper body off the floor, breathing in, keeping your thighs and pelvis on the ground. Unless you have neck problems, you should try to look up toward the ceiling.

Arch your back and stretch your upper body toward the ceiling as far as is comfortable; focus on lengthening your spine, not compressing it.

Unless your spine is very flexible, your arms will more than likely remain slightly bent. Hold this position for as long as is comfortable while breathing normally, maybe 20 seconds.

Breathing out, lower your upper body back to the ground. This is one round.

If you manage a good, long hold in the Cobra position, one round may be enough. If you can hold it only for a short time, two repetitions will be fine.

Benefits: A supple spine is a great gift, and the Cobra will help you get there. It also improves circulation in your back and tones the spinal nerves. It can stimulate digestion, can relieve constipation, and works the liver, kidney, and reproductive organs.

4. Forward Bending Pose

Instructions

Stand with your feet about a foot apart. Keep your knees straight. Breathe out and bend forward from your waist until you feel a deep stretch in your hamstrings. Don't force it. If you can touch your toes, go for it. If not, rest your hands on your knees or shins.

Hold this position for as long as is comfortable—20 seconds would be great—and breathe normally. Breathe in as you return to the standing position.

Benefits: Besides the hamstrings getting a good stretch, this pose works the abdomen and improves digestion. Like the Cobra, it works the spine and the spinal nerves and improves blood circulation.

5. Thunderbolt Pose

Instructions

Kneel on the floor and sit back on your heels. The heels should be separated, but the big toes of both feet should be touching.

Rest your bottom on the insides of your feet. The knees should remain together. Place your hands, palms down, on your knees.

Your spine and head should be straight, but relaxed—imagine a cord attached to the top of your head gently pulling you up. Look directly forward.

Close your eyes and relax, breathing normally.

Try to remain in the posture for at least 2 minutes.

Benefits: This posture stills the mind and strengthens the pelvic muscles. Most important, it aids digestion.

Mind Over Matter

Whether you're an adventure seeker, a get-up-and-go kinda girl, or a laid-back chick, you'll benefit from some of these motivational tools and techniques. Try them!

Okay, so you're not as fit as you'd like to be. Stop assessing things negatively. The fact that you're reading this book is a positive affirmation that you want to change. And now you have all the tools to begin that process. Try to see problems as opportunities and they won't get you down.

Focus on the present. A great deal of unhappiness comes from regretting the past and dreading the future. Ask yourself, "What Do I Need Today?" and wait for a spontaneous and intuitive response. This technique will bring your goals and dreams into the present.

When you're upset, think of something that you are grateful for. If you are able-bodied, be grateful for it and think of the people all over the planet who struggle for the privilege of walking or the leisure of exercise. It's impossible to feel bad about a situation when you experience gratitude.

Set reasonable goals. If you haven't done any exercise for a while it can be scary in the beginning. Start with a walk two or three days a week and slowly add a session or two of yoga. In time you'll feel more confident.

Begin an Exercise Diary. When you start out it's a great idea to schedule exercise into your week. Pencil in the times when you will be available for a stroll or some yoga. After a month or so, you'll be able to review your progress and slowly build in new and exciting exercise adventures.

Motivate yourself with some new sneakers. Make a point of throwing out your old ones. Your heels, ankles, back, and neck will thank you.

Get up earlier. Research shows that people who exercise early in the day stick to their routines. (I know it might mean going to bed earlier, which can be tough when you're studying for exams, but a little exercise will also help you perform better when you're under pressure.)

Go at your own pace. Focusing on what's right for your body (rather than anyone else's) will help you stick to your plan and eliminate self-defeating comparisons.

Don't daydream while you exercise. Being present in the exercise helps you enjoy it more. This focus also concentrates more on muscle use, making the workout more effective.

Bring a friend. Exercising with a buddy is a fun way to do your routine. And you can help motivate each other.

Push yourself without injuring yourself. There's a fine line between setting yourself up for an injury by going at it too hard and pushing yourself through a barrier. It's important to set exercise goals but remember to be flexible with these goals.

Don't exercise when you're sick. It will not only put you off your stride, it may harm your body.

Do what you enjoy and fitness will follow. If you love swimming, the chances are you'll do it more often than trying to stick to an exercise that's not really your thing.

Exercise Is Not a Luxury, It's a Necessity

Given all the PR juice on exercise, you may think that a little exercise is good but more would be better—not necessarily. Scientists now believe that people who push themselves extra hard during exercise may actually weaken their immune systems. Just a few Body Type–specific yoga postures, a gentle walk three times a week, and a few cardio-boosting sessions each week are enough to help stimulate your immune and cardiovascular systems and keep all your joints, muscles, tendons, and bones in good working order. As long as you do it regularly.

The perfect exercise program is one that's perfectly in tune with your nature. It demands nothing more than doing what feels right, when it feels right. And believe me, when you're in balance, you'll want to get out there, celebrate the gift of your body, and exercise regularly.

When our bodies are active we feel strong, confident, and in charge of our lives. Exercise allows us to breathe in fresh air, commune with nature, and take time out from school and chores to experience the bliss of our existence. *Exercise makes us feel good about ourselves and our bodies.* It fills us with energy and enthusiasm. And takes us out of the daily hassle of demanding parents, nagging teachers, school pressures, and friendship crises to connect us with our vital force. Possibly the most important thing about exercise is that it gives you direct access to GirlForce. So go, girl, you're ready to take up the fitness challenge.

Begin it now!

CHAPTER FIVE

Celebrate Your Unique Beauty

The **GirlForce beauty** mantra—keep it real! Very few of us have model bodies, **flawless skin**, and **perfect hair**. Nature intended us to be different, with **different shapes** and sizes and unique faces. One thing is universal, a **happy face** is a **beautiful** face. Let your **spirit shine** through your smile.

Understanding that each Body Type and each individual is beautiful in its own way is a huge part of what GirlForce is all about. You'll boost self-esteem and confidence when you find out what skin care routines, styles of clothing, colors, and jewelry will heal and balance YOU. Accepting your unique beauty as a gift of nature no matter what shape, size, or color you are releases your GirlForce.

BEAUTY IS MORE THAN SKIN DEEP.
A cliché perhaps, but true. There's much more to being beautiful than having a clothes-hanger body, perfect hair, and a conventionally pretty face. Beauty is something that comes from your spirit and your heart.

Because our society is so obsessed with images (pictures in magazines, music videos on TV), we only ever get to see the surfaces of people, not what's really going on inside. And it's what's going on inside that really counts. As a beauty editor, I have met some of the world's "most beautiful women"—celebrities,

models, and actresses—and, believe me, many of them are also the most insecure and unhappy people you could meet. They are constantly worried about how they look and how other people perceive them. Being obsessed about how you look all the time is a kind of prison that's really hard to escape from.

The key to feeling fab, inside and out, is looking after yourself. When you're really confident about how to manage and get on top of breakouts, bad hair days, broken nails, and wardrobe hang-ups, you're on your way to feeling great.

Air
Beauty

WHETHER YOU'RE STATUESQUE AND TALL or cute, cuddly, and petite, a quirky Air girl understands that beauty is in the eye of the beholder. Air girls are generally the most unusual looking of the three Body Types— their beauty comes from their uniqueness, and it's often said about an Air girl that "she's got a fascinating and intelligent face." Air girls can have high cheekbones, long or short yet graceful noses, an angular bone structure, and a face that could be said to be eye-catching and attention-grabbing. An Air girl's skin is often on the dry side, but she has fine, mostly clear skin that's the envy of her friends. Whether she has a smattering of freckles or no freckles at all, she can generally get a sun-kissed tan in next to no time when she's exposed to the sun. Her hair, well, the Air babe's hair is often one of her biggest beauty concerns: kinky, unruly, dry, and often fine and hard to manage. The Air girl is constantly shelling out bucks for hair products to manage her locks. She has a small, sweet mouth and often has cute little teeth. And her expressive eyes often dart from one thing to another, revealing the workings of her quick mind. She's one of a kind, and when she recognizes and celebrates her individuality, she's truly beautiful.

Quick Fixes for Air Trouble Spots

Dry skin

To super-hydrate your skin, especially during winter, once a week make up a mask using honey and rose essential oil. Drop six drops of the oil into about half an ounce of honey and paste the mixture onto your skin. You can team this treatment with a warm bath and lie back and relax. After 20 minutes, rinse off the mask. Your skin should feel warm, hydrated, and tingly.

Dandruff

To prevent dry, flaky scalp conditions, prepare an aromatherapy hair and scalp treatment. Add five drops of rosemary, two drops of tea tree, and one drop of lavender essential oil to half an ounce of olive oil and rub rigorously through your hair. Wash as normal with a gentle shampoo.

Frizzy hair

To nourish and calm dry, flyaway hair, make up a hair mask using yogurt and avocado. Mix the ingredients together and work into the hair. Put on a shower cap for 20 minutes to heat everything up so it infuses. Rinse out. Your hair should be shiny and manageable.

Air Beauty Tips

1. Use a moisturizer a.m. and p.m. **2.** Your lips
tend to dry out, so keep a lip balm handy. **3.** Use a
sunscreen daily. **4.** If your eyes need definition, rim them
with a little eyeliner and lashings of mascara. **5.** Keep out
of cold, dry environments as they dehydrate your skin.
6. Your color palette: if your skin is fair to pale, go for soft,
pastel pink for lips and cheeks; pale blue, lilac, and green
for eye shadow; lush pink and orange for nail polish.
Muted browns are grounding for Air while gold is
uplifting. If your skin is olive to dark, opt for
shimmering apricot for eyes and cheeks,
nude beige and silver for lips, and
pinks and oranges for nails.

Fire
Beauty

IN CLASSIC AYURVEDA, FIRE IS MARKED BY redness—either in hair or skin. Lindsay Lohan is a typical Fire chick, though not all Fire girls have pale skin. Girls with darker skin tones can still be prone to sensitivity and redness. Fire girls are often identified by their outdoorsy, healthy looks and their warm, soft skin. They tend to get burned if they sit in the sun, and freckles are a common feature of a Fire girl's complexion. She often has sparkling eyes, and when you're talking to her, it's the magnetic gaze you'll notice first—she seems to look right into your soul. Fire chicks often have thick hair, and it's likely to have a golden or red tint in it. Her most pressing beauty concern is her skin, which is prone to breakouts and sensitivity. Because fair Fire girls are prone to getting sunburned, their beauty weapon of choice must be sunscreen—don't leave home without it. Her lips are generally not super full, but her open, warm, and passionate smile is a killer. The Fire chick is generally Miss Confidence when it comes to her looks. Even if she's not a supermodel, she can look in the mirror and feel okay about her appearance. She's a scene-stealer with a rosy glow, which is positively babelicious.

Fire Beauty
Tips

1. Use a moisturizer a.m. and p.m. **2.** Keep out of the sun and always wear sunscreen. **3.** If you have fair eyebrows and lashes, use a soft brown pencil to color the eyebrows and give them definition, and use brown mascara to lick on the lashes. **4.** Use a fragrance-free daily moisturizer. Fragrances can irritate sensitive Fire complexions. **5.** Opt for foundations that include sun filters as they'll boost your UV protection. **6.** Your color palette: if your skin is pale to fair and freckled, opt for cool colors such as lime, pale blue, aqua, and white for the eyes. Try gorgeous fuchsias and purples for the lips and dusky pinks and oranges for the cheeks and nails. If your skin is olive to black, avoid red, yellow, and brown shades and select shimmering pinks, sky blues, and lime green for eyes and frosted glossy oranges and bright golds for cheeks and nails. Anything sparkly will give you a chic finish.

Quick Fixes for Fire Trouble Spots

Sensitive skin

To calm and soothe red, irritated skin buy fresh coconut oil from the health food store and apply it to your face, scalp, and body. Rinse off in the shower. The oil cools the skin and helps prevent irritation.

Oily T-zone

Keep the skin balanced and nourished; moisturize daily and do a weekly exfoliation treatment with a mixture of oatmeal, honey, and milk. Mix this up into a paste and apply it to the face. Rub in small circular movements over the T-zone and rinse off using cold water. This mask tones and tightens the pores, leaving your skin feeling clean and fresh.

Sunburn

Fire skin can burn easily, so it's essential to use an SPF 30 sunscreen for all outdoor activity. If the skin gets burned, the best idea is to soak in a cool-to-warm bath with fifteen drops of lavender essential oil. The lavender soothes the burn and helps reduce inflammation. Yogurt can also be put on the skin to reduce the effects of the burn.

Perspiration and odor

If you tend to get smelly feet, the best thing to do is sprinkle a couple of drops of sweet-smelling lavender essential oil into your shoes. Lavender is antibacterial and helps stop the odor from building up. If you've noticed your armpits are getting a bit funky, especially after working out, try using a tea tree oil deodorant. You can get it from your local health food store.

Zits

Once a zit appears with a head (black or white), the best thing to do is soften the pimple with a warm compress (get a wash cloth and wet it with warm water). Keep the compress on the spot for a minute or so, then get a tissue and, with both index fingers, squeeze the pimple; try to get under the zit without pressing too hard. Once the head has popped, dab a drop of tea tree oil on the spot with a cotton ball. Then leave it alone. Don't pick it!

Earth Beauty

LUSH AND CURVY EARTH BABES are blessed with a serene nature that's often reflected in their faces. Characterized by large, sleepy eyes with thick, long lashes, the Earth girl has a gentle beauty that's all her own. She often has thick, wavy hair, and she's generally pale for her race. She also has bright white teeth and the whites of her eyes are also super-white. Large, full Angelina Jolie lips are an Earth trait, and when an Earth girl slicks on a little gloss to make the most of them, she's positively kissable. Oily skin and oily hair are the most pressing beauty issues, but she can also get deep zits that refuse to budge, as well as the odd blackhead. Generally Earth girls are on the voluptuous side, so they need to resist the temptation to beat themselves up for being bigger than their Air and Fire girlfriends. Once they realize they have a feminine beauty that's considered cool in many parts of the world, they glow. Attitude is what it's all about.

Earth Beauty Tips

1. If you have slightly oily skin, you may be tempted to try to dry it out and starve it of moisture. Instead keep it hydrated by using a light moisturizer daily or use a blend of nourishing essential oils such as three drops of geranium and three drops of rose in half an ounce of sweet almond oil. Skip the night cream. **2.** Wear sunscreen daily. **3.** Exercise is one way to keep the Earth skin glowing. Regular aerobic exercise will bring a healthy flush to the cheeks. **4.** A daily face massage is great to help relieve any puffiness under the eyes. **5.** Your eyes are probably your most seductive feature. Bring attention to them with lashings of black or blue mascara. **6.** Your color palette: if your skin is pale, go for warm and stimulating colors such as red, orange, gold, dark brown, and purple. Darker-skinned girls will find their lush looks are enhanced with dazzling berry gloss, metallic shades of bronze and gold, and iridescent shadows and powders. Whatever your skin tone, from fair to olive to black, avoid wishy-washy pastel shades.

Quick Fixes for Earth Trouble Spots

Open pores and blackheads

The best way to keep the skin toned, tight, and fresh is to do regular exfoliation treatments. Ground almond meal (you can get it from the health food store) mixed with yogurt and honey makes a fab scrub. Do this once a week and apply a light oil-free moisturizer after the treatment.

Oily skin

One of the smartest ways to control oil is, paradoxically, with oil. Before going to bed use a mixture of half an ounce of sweet almond oil mixed with three drops of lavender, two drops of chamomile, and one drop of geranium essential oils. The blend will help nourish and hydrate the skin and minimize oil slick.

Blind pimples

A simple way to encourage blind zits to come to a head is to apply a compress of red clay (from the health food store) to the spot and let the clay dry. The clay draws impurities to the surface. Once the pimple has formed a head, squeeze gently with a tissue and apply tea tree or lavender essential oil.

GirlForce Beauty Essentials for Every Body

It's all about the way you think about it. Looking after yourself can be a chore or it can be a complete and utter pleasure. You choose.

THINK IT'S ENOUGH to keep your skin, hair, and nails clean? Think again. Doing the basics—washing your hair, wiping away the raccoon eyes from the night before, and rubbing in a moisturizer—are the bare minimum if you want to look and feel great. I'm not trying to stress you with a million routines, but your daily beauty rituals are some of the best chances you have in a busy life to nurture and pamper yourself.

Self-pampering is really important for your health and well-being. When you massage a moisturizer into your skin or wash your hair with aromatherapy shampoos, you send a rush of feel-good chemicals like adrenaline through your system. And because this pampering is a gift you give yourself, it majorly boosts your self-esteem. Basic grooming routines can all become self-pampering sessions when you become aware of how good these self-nurturing practices can be.

It's up to you how often you use these self-pampering tools, but it's worth noting that the more you do them, the better you'll feel. (And by the way, you can share the bliss by giving a friend an aromatherapy massage or a deluxe healing facial. Spread the pampering pleasure around.)

Aromatherapy

Essential oils are powerful healing chemicals that come from plants, fruits, and flowers. They've been used for centuries to help de-stress the mind, body, and spirit through a yummy combo of touch and smell. If you use them as part of your daily self-pampering rituals you'll discover a new path to peace.

The healing powers of essential oils can be experienced through being stroked onto the skin with massage, dropped into the bath, scattered on clean sheets, or vaporized into the atmosphere.

One of the main aims of aromatherapy is to discover ways and means of getting essential oils to penetrate the body. When they enter the bloodstream, they act on the vital systems of the body such as the central nervous system, the lymphatic system, the muscles, tissues, and the brain. And by boosting the body's own defense mechanisms via touch and smell, aromatherapy helps restore balance and vitality.

Body Type Oils

Essential oils can also be used to balance the elemental-energies in your Body Type.

One more word on essential oils. It's important to buy genuine essential oils rather than fragrant oils that are synthetic and made in a laboratory. Essential oils have healing properties because they're straight from Mother Nature. They're strong, so go easy with them (stick to my instructions about dosages and don't apply them directly on the skin unless it's in tiny amounts, like a dab here and there on a zit).

Essential oils are sometimes more expensive than synthetic oils, but they're worth saving up for because they're the real deal.

Which Essential Oils Are Right for Your Type?

Air: Go for these essential oils—clove, orange, basil, geranium, frankincense, jasmine, neroli, sandalwood, patchouli, chamomile, and rose.

Fire: Go for these essential oils—jasmine, sandalwood, vetiver, peppermint, lavender, ylang-ylang, cedarwood, lemongrass, lemon, and tea tree.

Earth: Go for these essential oils—patchouli, geranium, eucalyptus, lavender, bergamot, mandarin, orange, grapefruit, lemon, cinnamon, and rose.

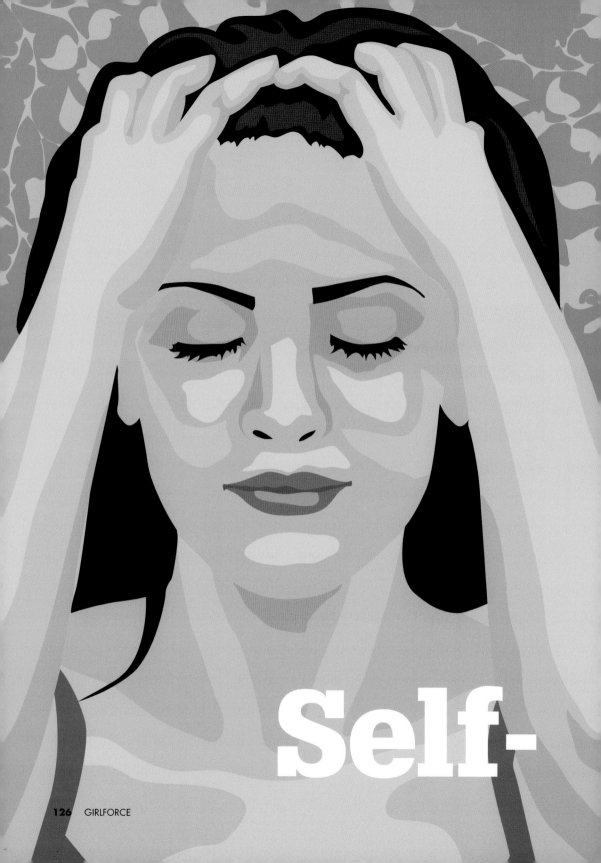

Self-

Step 1. The Scalp

In Ayurvedic healing, there's a point on the top of the head, about eight finger-widths above the eyebrows, which is the place where energy leaves the body. It's the soft spot that remains on the scalp from birth, and it's known as the seat of bliss. This is where your massage begins. Apply oil to the palm of your hand and gently pat or stroke the point, applying light, even pressure.

- Grab the hair growing over the point, giving it a gentle twist to stimulate the nerves. Finally, give a little tug and release.
- Use your fingertips to massage over the entire surface of the scalp.
- Allow your thumbs to press into the deep indentation at the base of the skull bone just above the hairline at the back of the neck. This is the place that energy is said to enter the body before birth.

There's no mystery to massage—anyone can do it—and by using this basic technique you can create your own personal brand of healing.

ACCORDING TO AYURVEDA, SELF-MASSAGE or "abhyanga" is an essential part of daily life. It's a totally wholistic treatment because it not only rids the body of stress and tension, it also encourages the flow of GirlForce through the body, mind, and spirit. The massage involves eight steps covering the whole body.

If you want to use oil, try cooling coconut oil if you're a Fire Type, nourishing olive oil if you're an Air Type, and stimulating sesame oil if you're an Earth Type. About 1 tablespoon should cover your whole body. Leave the oil on as long as possible (a minimum of 20 minutes would be great), and when you're ready to get dressed, rinse off in a warm shower with a gentle soap.

massage

Step 2. The Feet

- Massage the right foot completely, covering it in oil.
- Using an even pressure, massage in an upward direction toward the heart. Repeat with the left foot.
- To relax and stimulate the feet, massage the inner arch of the foot moving your thumb in circular motions. This movement stimulates the heart.
- Massage the point located on the underside of your big toe, pressing gently with your thumb. (This point helps regulate your hormonal systems.)
- Using your thumb and fingers, massage all around the base of each toe and gently pull upward from the base to the tip. According to Ayurveda, each toe, from the biggest to the smallest, corresponds to a major organ: brain, lungs, intestines, kidney, and heart.
- Using both hands, massage the foot in upward strokes from the toes to the ankles.

Step 3. The Legs

- Do one leg at a time.
- Start with the right ankle and wrap both hands around the joint and massage in a clockwise direction.
- From the ankle, massage up the calf and shin in upward and downward strokes, covering the surface of the lower leg in oil.
- Massage the fronts of the knees in circular motions and gently massage the backs of the knees in a clockwise motion.
- Massage up and down the thighs from the knees to the groin using upward and downward strokes.
- Cover the thigh in oil and, using your knuckles, gently rub the back

of the upper thighs near the buttocks in small circular motions.

Step 4. The Arms

- Do one arm at a time.
- Start with the right arm and cover the length of the arm with oil then massage the palm.
- Using your thumb in circular movements in the center of the palm, press the point gently and evenly.
- Starting with the thumb, massage each finger working from the base of the finger to the tip. Lightly tug each finger.
- Massage the top side of the hand from the fingers to the wrist.
- Work up and down the lower arm from the wrist to the elbow.
- Massage up and down the upper arm into the armpit and over the shoulder.

Step 5. The Back

- It's pretty hard to massage your own back, but the more you practice self-massage the more flexible you will become, making it easier to reach your back, shoulders, and bottom.
- . Using the palms of your hands, massage up and down the lower back, stimulating the spine with your thumbs as you work up and down.
- Using your thumbs and index fingers, grab the flesh on the middle to lower back (as far up as you can reach) and use a grab and release motion as you work up and down the spine.
- To massage the shoulders and upper back, rub your palms over the areas. If you have trouble reaching use a rolled up towel and hold onto

According to Ayurveda, self-massage or "abhyanga" is an essential part of daily life. It's a totally wholistic treatment because it not only rids the body of stress and tension, it also encourages the flow of GirlForce through the body, mind, and spirit.

each end rubbing it over the surface of your back.

Step 6. The Abdomen
- Pour oil directly onto the belly button area.
- With your fingers, gently massage the navel in clockwise circles.
- Using your palm, slowly radiate the circles outward to cover the entire belly.
- Reverse the direction, making the circles smaller as you rotate the palm toward the belly button.

Step 7. The Upper Body
- Using alternate hands, massage the upper area of the chest in clockwise motions, working around the breasts, avoiding the nipples.
- Work in a figure eight around the entire upper chest.

Step 8. The Face and Neck
- With both hands, lightly stroke up and down the neck, covering it with oil.
- Using your fingers, walk them up the back of the neck, finishing just under the base of the skull.
- Start on the face by covering the skin in oil.
- With a light, even pressure, place your index finger on the point between the upper lip and the nose,

then place your middle finger between the lower lip and chin. Use both hands.
- Using a sweeping movement, glide the fingers (which are making a peace sign) away from the center of the face toward the ears. Massage the right and left sides at the same time using this action.
- Using the fingertips, sweep up from the base of the nose toward the temples.
- After you've massaged the cheeks, follow with the eye area. Using your middle fingers, press the points under your eyebrows next to the top of the nose. Sweep your fingers along the brow line and make a circle around the eye sockets, finishing with a gentle press at the start of the eyebrows.
- Massage the eyebrow center with the middle fingers, pressing in small clockwise circles around the center of the brow.
- Place your middle fingers on the tip of the nose and sweeping up over the nose and forehead continue stroking the skin toward the hairline.
- Finish the massage by stroking across the forehead with the fingers, using the right hand to stroke from left to right, then alternate using the left hand to stroke from right to left.

Dress for Success

Some people are born with red carpet style.
They can throw together a pair of jeans and a
vintage jacket and look like a million bucks.
Other people, well, they need a bit of help. Far
be it from me to tell you how to dress—you'll
have your own personal style, and you'll be
the best judge of what looks hot on you and
what doesn't. But there are some style
maxims that relate to your Body Type that
might just surprise you.

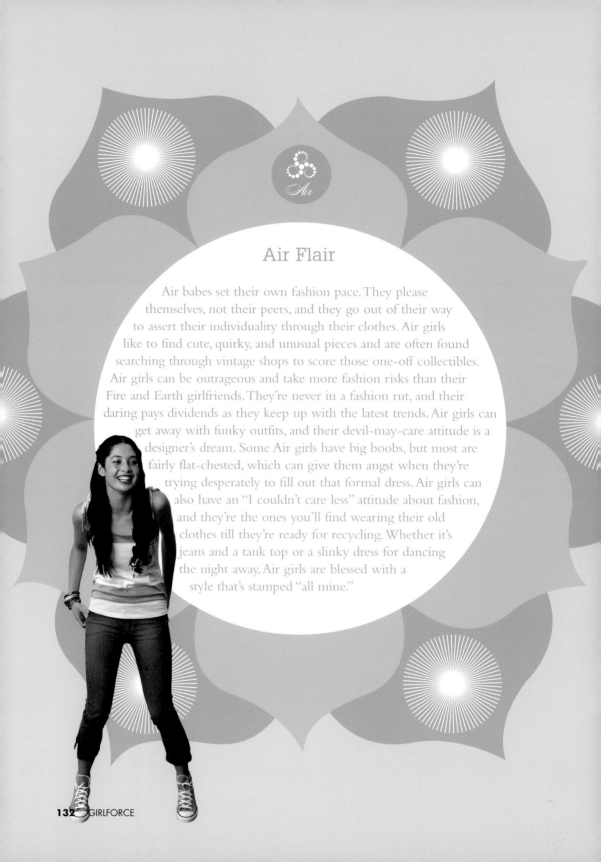

Air Flair

Air babes set their own fashion pace. They please themselves, not their peers, and they go out of their way to assert their individuality through their clothes. Air girls like to find cute, quirky, and unusual pieces and are often found searching through vintage shops to score those one-off collectibles. Air girls can be outrageous and take more fashion risks than their Fire and Earth girlfriends. They're never in a fashion rut, and their daring pays dividends as they keep up with the latest trends. Air girls can get away with funky outfits, and their devil-may-care attitude is a designer's dream. Some Air girls have big boobs, but most are fairly flat-chested, which can give them angst when they're trying desperately to fill out that formal dress. Air girls can also have an "I couldn't care less" attitude about fashion, and they're the ones you'll find wearing their old clothes till they're ready for recycling. Whether it's jeans and a tank top or a slinky dress for dancing the night away, Air girls are blessed with a style that's stamped "all mine."

Style Tips

- Don't worry if you're a bit on the skinny side, make the most of your angular shape and go for close-fitting jeans and body-hugging tees.
- If you're flat-chested, don't go for plunging necklines, but don't spend all your cash on Wonderbras either. Celebrate your boobs, no matter how big or small they are.
- If you have large breasts, you'll look great in simple dresses in bold colors.
- You like to be at the cutting edge, but sometimes it's good to save up for more classic pieces and good-quality accessories that last for years. Your unique, edgy, sometimes outrageous style is totally cool.

Fire Style

Fire girls love to be the center of attention, so by
the time they've hit their teens, they know how to
turn heads. Whether they go for a sporty, casual, outdoorsy
style or a hipper, sleeker fashion groove, they're the girls who
know how to work their assets. Normally athletic, the
Fire girl is comfortable hanging around in jeans,
T-shirts, and sneakers. She's also a natural flirt and knows
how to put together a sexy outfit for partying. (When
she's hot, she sizzles.) She's not a quirky dresser like her
Air pals; instead, she likes to be hip, cool, and trendy.
Her personal style can be classic and girlie at times,
but the natural tomboy within likes to get out and
go crazy. She's comfy in chic and sophisticated, but
she's equally at ease in sweatpants or a simple
sarong. She knows she's a babe, and she's not
afraid to flaunt it. Fire girls love to push the
limits with their clothes and need to be
careful that they don't go too over
the top.

Style Tips

- You tend to like sexy yet classy clothes that show off your toned physique, but be careful not to go overboard with too much bling— sometimes it's better to dress down than up.
- You look great in outdoorsy casual and posh party dresses. Make the most of your assets by wearing chic, simple pieces that can be teamed with bling and a cool pair of shoes.
- Save up for a great jacket that will go with cargoes or a slip dress; a hip jacket is a must for any wardrobe.
- If you have red or pinkish undertones in your skin, red, yellow, and orange can make your complexion look flushed. Go for blues, greens, and white. Can you think of anything cooler than jeans and a cute tank top?

Earth Glamour

Earth girls are the most conservative of the three types. Their classic tastes and innate refinement prompts them to buy beautiful clothes that last. Unlike their Air friends who buy clothes only to ditch them one season later, Earth girls like to collect clothes that hang in their wardrobes for seasons. Not being the skinny minis of the class, Earth girls can be frustrated by fashion. But when they get into their curves, they present a polished style that is sophisticated and sassy. Earth girls can look older than their years, generally because they've developed breasts and a butt before everyone else. But these feminine bits can be turned into assets when Earth girls know how to dress for their shape. (It's cool when Earth girls realize that you don't have to be super trendy to be hot. When you're confident about your fashion sense, anything goes.) Earth girls can get into fashion ruts, so every now and again, it's a good idea to toss out everything in the wardrobe and start again.

Style Tips

- Earth girls take note! Don't be afraid to flaunt your curves. I'm not suggesting you should go all sexy-smoldering, but don't cover up your shape with overly baggy clothes either.
- Flat shoes can make fuller Earth shapes look a bit frumpy, even if you're tall, so wear a kitten heel with dresses and add a little height when you're wearing pants.
- A-line skirts are a must for Earth girls; team with a body-hugging tee.
- Save up and buy good bras with built-in support.
- Don't overdo patterns or too much jewelry—keep it simple. Sweet!

Jewelry That's Right for Your Body Type

Cultivating a passion for bling-bling? Longing for diamonds and pearls? Every girl does! Use gem stones and precious metals to balance your Body Type.

- Ruby and garnet balance Air and Earth, help improve circulation and digestion, and strengthen the heart.
- Pearl, moonstone, and milky quartz balance Fire and Air, help nourish the body, and decrease anxiety.
- Emerald, jade, and peridot balance Air and Fire, promote healing, help strengthen the lungs, and balance the nervous system.
- Yellow sapphire, yellow topaz, citrine, and amber balance Air and help increase energy and regulate the hormones.
- Diamond, clear quartz, blue sapphire, blue topaz, turquoise, and aquamarine balance Air, Fire, and Earth and help protect against negative energy.
- Opal balances Earth and Air and helps increase compassion and understanding.
- Jet and smoky quartz balance Earth and help protect against negativity.
- Gold balances Air, Fire, and Earth and harmonizes the energies in the body, mind, and spirit.
- Silver balances Fire and helps cool and calm the emotions.

You're a Natural-Born Beauty

You've got what it takes to be on top of the world. You're free, you're young, you're hip, and you're in sync with your Body Type. **It pays to remember that whether you're Air, Fire, or Earth, you're unique and gorgeous in your own way. No two Body Types are alike. Even if all your girlfriends are Fire Types, you'll notice that they're all totally one-of-a-kind and beautiful because they're different from everyone else.**

When you discover the joys of your unique beauty, no one will ever be able to put you down. Why? Because beauty is all about confidence. And if you're on the shy side, don't stress—living a GirlForce life will give you the confidence to carry off whatever it is you'd like to wear. Imagine you're pumped full of GirlForce energy, and then put on the makeup, jewelry, and clothes that you love, feeling awesome. Being beautiful is as simple as that.

CHAPTER SIX

The Lowdown on Stress

Stress sucks. But you don't have to **live** with it. Here's how to **take control** of your angst before it takes control of **you**.

Freaking out about the size of your butt, being traumatized about what to wear, worrying about exams, being dumped by boys and hassled by your peers are all pretty standard girl dilemmas. But how you deal on those scores depends a lot on your Body Type. Find out what factors increase stress for your Body Type and check out how you can chill out.

THERE'S NOT A PERSON ON THE PLANET who doesn't get stressed. Even the super-cool Miss Popularity types, who appear not to sweat it like the rest of us, get stressed. Stress is part and parcel of living, but it doesn't have to ruin your life. Meditation, yoga, exercise, and eating right for your Body Type are all practices that will help you get your angst under control.

It's definitely time to give up stressing about the little things. Like what you're going to wear to impress that hottie you saw at the bus stop or how to handle the zit that's burning on your chin. Get a grip, girl! There are bigger things in life to worry about. There are things in life that are worthy of serious consideration. Like being bullied at school. Or being dissed by your best friend, and even more hard-core, it's really tough to deal with the breakdown of your family, drug and alcohol problems, or sex abuse.

We're talking about stress here, and probably the most important thing to realize about stress is that it's all in your mind. Okay, it's in your body too—who hasn't felt butterflies before a big party or tense muscles before a semifinal? Stress is a personal response to a situation. It's not the situation itself that causes stress, it's your response to it that makes your heart beat faster and your palms sweat. This is the reason why some people are invigorated and hyped by the thought of parachuting out of an airplane while others are terrified to the point of paralysis. One girl's stress is another girl's party.

Your Body Type has a huge influence on how you handle and approach stress. When Air girls get stressed, they think too much. They lie awake at night worrying until they're twisted up in knots. Fire girls can get short-fused when they're angsting over something, and Earth girls, well, they just get insular and moody when they're worried.

Psychologists generally agree there are two types of stress: acute stress, which is short-term stress caused by the impact of a stressful life event such as exams or a fight with your crush; and chronic stress, which is long-term stress, like your parents having an ugly breakup.

Most people can deal with some degree of acute stress; in fact, a little stress can be a positive and powerful force. What many doctors and psychologists are discovering is that far too many of us are trapped in a negative cycle of chronic stress. Factors such as relentless bullying, an illness in the family, or being sexually abused may cause chronic stress.

Chronic stress is very hard to treat and there are no quick fixes. The current thinking is that once you can identify the things that "personally" stress you out, then you're in a much better position to manage your reaction to them.

When we are stressed, everything suffers—our homework, our relationships, our skin, our health, our clarity of mind, and even our society. What matters is how well you handle it. It's time for each and every one of us to get a grip.

GirlForce Defeats Stress

Ever heard the old adage "Practice makes perfect"? When it comes to stress, the practice of living in tune with your Body Type helps you reach a perfect state of happiness, confidence, and peace. The daily habit of eating, exercising, meditating, pampering, and dressing in a way that balances your Body Type helps defeat stress.

It means that you don't really have to do anything "extra" to manage your stress; you just have to use your daily routines as a way to stay calm, peaceful, and in harmony with yourself and the universe. If you push people to go cold turkey on their addictions, negative habits, and behaviors in one big hit, that in itself causes stress. *The best way to combat stress is to add activities and thoughts that promote wellness, happiness, and peace one at a time, leaving less room for the stuff that stresses you out.*

Of course it's easier said than done. We develop addictions to substances such as alcohol, cigarettes, coffee, junk food, drugs, and sex to comfort ourselves and help us cope with full-tilt stress. Addictions also tend to complement each other—many people smoke and drink alcohol or watch lots of television and eat junk food. But if you can introduce just one GirlForce-enhancing practice into your life—and it doesn't matter which one—you'll have a better chance of breaking the downward spiral of a stress-producing lifestyle. The more you add health-creating habits to your life, the easier it is to let go of the substances, stressors, and behaviors that can harm you.

How Stressed Are You?

ANXIETY, DEPRESSION, PAIN, INSOMNIA, chronic fatigue, and aggression are all by-products of stress. Most people suffer from some of these symptoms at some point, which is normal. Stress becomes problematic when it becomes chronic and long-term. It's important to assess just how stressed you are, so you can develop strategies to beat it.

The following test, "How Stressed Are You?," is designed to give you an indicator of how stress is affecting you.

You may find you're more stressed than you imagine. Or, good news, you may work out that you're handling the stresses in your life like an ace. "How Stressed Are You?" will reveal your overall mental and emotional stress. It will help you develop awareness of your stress levels, so you can be honest with yourself about the steps you need to take to combat the bad effects of stress on your body, mind, and spirit. Those steps, including meditation, creative visualization, and yummy pampering practices, are outlined later in this chapter in the Stress Management Plans for your Body Type.

Read through the following statements and respond with a simple yes or no.

1. I'm having problems with relationships.
2. I'm finding it difficult to sleep.
3. I worry a lot of the time.
4. Right now, I'm experiencing a major change in my school or home environment.
5. I'm desperate for a vacation.
6. I'm stressing about a teacher, parent, or friend.
7. I'm freaking out about the amount of homework per week.
8. I'm not doing much exercise.
9. I'm skipping meals.
10. I'm using TV or the computer as a way to escape reality.
11. I'm often fearful of the future.
12. I'm snappy at brothers and sisters, friends, and parents.
13. I never get to relax.
14. My sense of humor has gone to dust. I can't see the funny side of life.
15. I expect to be super-successful at everything.
16. I'm feeling overwhelmed a lot of the time.
17. I've been diagnosed with a chronic health condition.
18. I'm finding it hard to concentrate.
19. I think I'm ugly.
20. No one likes me.

ADD UP YOUR SCORE

SCORE 1 FOR YES AND 0 FOR NO

IF YOU SCORED 1–5

Awesome. You're in great shape. You have few hassles in your life, and you're handling the ones you have. Be careful not to be so laid-back that you avoid challenges because they appear too stressful. You will increase your chances of maintaining your laid-back attitude to life if you begin a meditation program and maintain a program of balancing your Body Type.

IF YOU SCORED 5–10

So you have many things in your life under control, but you may have experienced an acute or short-term stress that has increased your score. Make sure that your lifestyle choices support your health and well-being. Eat, exercise, meditate, and dress in ways to balance your Body Type and you should be in great shape.

IF YOU SCORED 10–15

It's time for you to take action and eliminate some big stresses from your life. Your health may already be under pressure and you may be discovering your relationships are suffering due to your pent-up emotions. Now would be a good time to take up some regular exercise and look at your diet and lifestyle. Include regular R&R breaks in your daily life and begin a consistent meditation program. Think seriously about doing the Stress Management Plan for your Body Type for a couple of weeks. Don't beat yourself up but do take action and discover ways to chill out.

IF YOU SCORED 15 AND OVER

Definitely time to stress down! It's possible that your health and well-being are suffering under the extreme stress you are experiencing. Time to build in some meditation, yoga, and R&R in your daily life, and I mean DAILY. Whether the stress is acute or chronic, you may need to seek the advice of a doctor or trusted counselor to talk through the things that are freaking you out. Use the Stress Management Plan for your Body Type, but whatever you do, don't wait any longer to address the stress in your life and seek professional help for whatever it is that's getting you down.

Stress and Your Body Type

Your Body Type reveals many of the secrets to the kinds of activities, foods, and events that may cause stress in your body and mind. While your reaction to any stress is unique, some things can cause more or less stress and strain according to your Body Type. For example, competitive sports might be a bit stressful for Air Types while they can be stimulating and fun for an Earth Type. Once you know the kinds of stresses that your Body Type is predisposed to, you can take active steps to eliminate them from your life.

While stress affects all levels of your being—mind, body, and spirit—you'll find that the kinds of things that relate to Body Type stress are mostly lifestyle factors such as diet, leisure, and physical activity. You'll also find that if *you deal with the stressors that relate to your Body Type first* it will create the space for a deeper awareness about the mental and emotional stressors affecting you.

Air Stress Management Plan

WHILE AIR GIRLS ARE CREATIVE, adventurous, and exciting to be around, they can also be sensitive and are particularly susceptible to Air stress symptoms such as anxiety, palpitations, irritable bowel syndrome, butterflies in the tummy, feeling faint, cold hands and feet, bad dreams, and insomnia. Poor diet, lack of regular gentle exercise, feeling overworked, prolonged worry or fear, and windy weather all deplete your GirlForce causing the Air elemental-energy to become imbalanced and the potential for stress and imbalance to manifest. If you're an Air girl and you scored higher than 10 in the "How Stressed Are You?" test, the following strategies will help you find balance and happiness.

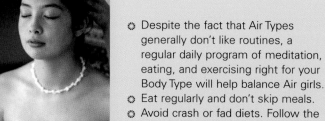

- Despite the fact that Air Types generally don't like routines, a regular daily program of meditation, eating, and exercising right for your Body Type will help balance Air girls.
- Eat regularly and don't skip meals.
- Avoid crash or fad diets. Follow the Air Nutritional Balancing Guide in Chapter Three.
- Do daily meditation and yoga.
- Exercise regularly, but do it gently.
- Do regular Creative Visualization.
- Take regular relaxation breaks.
- Take lots of warm baths and give yourself massages and pampering treats.
- Air is a dry and cold energy. To keep it in balance, make sure you stay warm yet not too dry. Sip warm or hot water during the day.
- I know you have to take exams and cope with loads of homework, but Air girls need to avoid as much mental and emotional strain as possible.

- Boost your self-confidence with regular affirmations and keep a GirlForce Experience Diary.
- Avoid loud music, late-night television, and violent movies— they all make the delicate Air elemental-energy crazy.
- Create a light, clean, harmonious bedroom. Air is balanced with sunlight and bright colors.
- Wear clothes with warm, stimulating tones: gold, yellow, pink, bright green, and pastels.
- Stimulants such as alcohol, cigarettes, caffeine, and drugs all upset the Air elemental-energy and deplete GirlForce. All Body Types benefit from the restriction of these substances; however, Air Types are particularly susceptible to the adverse effects of these stimulants.
- The essential oils of clove, orange, basil, frankincense, jasmine, neroli, sandalwood, patchouli, chamomile, and rose balance and harmonize the Air elemental-energy. Drop no more than ten drops of a blend or single oil into a warm bath or into a vaporizer.

Fire Stress Management Plan

FIRE TYPES ARE THE MOST LIKELY to suffer the symptoms of burnout. Typical symptoms of Fire-related stress are anger, irritability, heartburn, skin rashes, sensitivity to heat and light, and a general feeling of heat in the body.

Feeling overworked, eating too many hot, spicy foods, sunburn, too much competition at school or home, drinking too many energy drinks or stimulants like caffeine, lack of regular Body Type balancing exercise, or long bouts of anger and aggressive behavior will deplete GirlForce and send the Fire elemental-energy into a state of chaos. If you are a high-octane Fire girl and scored higher than 10 in the "How Stressed Are You?" test, the following strategies will help you find calm and contentment.

- Coolness in any form helps combat Fire stress. Maintaining a cool room temperature is as important as keeping the emotions cool.
- Drink plenty of cool (not cold) liquids during the day. Favor sweet-tasting drinks but avoid carbonated drinks.
- Follow the Fire Nutritional Balancing Guide in Chapter Three.
- Do regular Fire balancing exercise, but don't overdo it.
- Do daily meditation and yoga practice.
- Calm the mind and body with Creative Visualization.
- Take regular breaks for relaxation and have fun.
- Start a GirlForce Experience Diary.
- Go swimming or take a cool bath or shower when you are overheated.
- I know you have to do exams and have tons of homework, but it's good for Fire girls to avoid working on long projects without breaks.
- Take regular breaks during the day. Go for a walk during your lunch hour, rather than gossiping or doing homework.
- Avoid stimulants; coffee, tea, cigarettes, drugs, and alcohol can all turn up the volume on the internal fire causing nervousness, irritability, and digestive problems.
- Eat regularly. Fire Types can become incredibly irritated when they are hungry. Skipping meals or eating late can cause the Fire elemental-energy to become imbalanced.
- Have massages, facials, and other healing therapies as often as possible—share and swap treatments with your girlfriends.
- Do some gentle self-massage daily with calming oils, such as coconut or olive oil.

- Wear clothes with cooling shades: aqua, blue, green, and silver.
- Fire is balanced with a cool environment. Keep your bedroom open, free of clutter, serene, and painted in pastel shades.
- Essential oils such as jasmine, sandalwood, vetiver, peppermint, and ylang-ylang will help cool and calm the Fire elemental-energy. Put no more than ten drops of a blend or single oil into a cool bath, sprinkle over clean sheets, or wear as a perfume.

Earth Stress Management Plan

BY NATURE, EARTH BEAUTIES TEND to be laid-back and serene. Of all the Body Types, Earth girls are less susceptible to stress than either Fire or Air. This doesn't mean they are immune to worry or fear. When Earth gals are stressed they tend to have symptoms such as weight gain, lethargy, depression, colds and flu, possessiveness, cravings for sweet and fatty foods, and digestive problems.

Lack of regular Body Type balancing exercise, cold and damp weather, long periods of inactivity, fatty foods, cold drinks, mental lethargy, and spiritual angst will all deplete GirlForce and aggravate the Earth elemental-energy.

If you're an Earth angel and scored higher than 10 in the "How Stressed Are You?" test, the following strategies will stimulate you into action and vitality.

- Earth is essentially a cool, damp energy, so it is best to avoid these conditions. Warmth and stimulation are key to keeping this elemental-energy in balance. A brisk walk in the sunlight is balancing for this elemental-energy and will awaken the creative passions.
- The Earth elemental-energy is slow to become imbalanced, but it is also slow to recover balance. The key to managing this elemental-energy is to keep it active and engaged; dullness in the mind and body is the enemy of the Earth elemental-energy.
- When an Earth girl is out of balance, she is prone to become housebound. Adventure, travel, and variety in life will prevent Earth stress from accumulating.
- Eating a light diet is essential for the Earth Type. Follow the Earth Nutritional Balancing Guide in Chapter Three.

- Regular Earth balancing exercise is a key to reducing stress. Of all the Types, Earth girls benefit the most from regular, rigorous exercise.
- Stimulate your mind with affirmation techniques and Creative Visualization.
- Keep a GirlForce Experience Diary.
- Do daily meditation and yoga practice.
- Wear clothes with earthy, stimulating tones: red, brown, gold, hot pink, and olive green.
- Perform daily self-massages with stimulating oils, such as almond or apricot kernel oil.
- Deep tissue massage, reflexology, and shiatsu will all help balance the Earth elemental-energy.
- Earth is invigorated when exposed to beauty. Make sure your bedroom is attractive and clean and filled with beautiful objects and paintings.
- Earth stress will often manifest itself as depression and fatigue. It's important to keep Earth stress at bay by talking to friends and parents about your troubles.
- Essential oils like patchouli, eucalyptus, lavender, bergamot, mandarin, orange, grapefruit, lemon, cinnamon, and rose help stimulate and balance the Earth elemental-energy. No more than ten drops of these oils, in a base of sweet almond oil and rubbed into the skin in massage or inhaled through the air or dropped into a hot bath, will energize and activate the Earth elemental-energy.

GirlForce-Boosting Anti-stress Strategies for Everyone

Now that you've done the "How Stressed Are You?" test, you'll have a very good idea of how stress is affecting you. And you've also discovered how you can correct many imbalances by following the Stress Management Plan for your Body Type.

Included in the Stress Management Plans for Air, Fire, and Earth are suggestions for pampering and nurturing therapies, such as aromatherapy and self-massage (you can check out Chapter Five), plus meditation and visualization practices. Don't stress—you are about to discover the secrets of the most powerful self-healing you can get your hands on.

Madonna does it every day. Drew and Demi swear by it. Meditation literally dissolves stress. It fills you with GirlForce and allows you to calm down, chill out, and feel totally cool.

Meditation Defeats Stress

Meditation is an age-old practice that's essentially designed to help us chill. There are literally thousands of meditation practices, but the whole point is to increase your energy, clear your mind, and shrink your stress.

Despite what many cynics may think, the practice of meditation does not require giving up your lifestyle or the fun things you enjoy. In fact, meditation is so accessible that it could be called the ultimate take-anywhere anti-stress strategy. So long as you have 10 to 20 minutes of peace and quiet, it can be done any place you happen to be.

The ideal is to practice 20 minutes twice a day, but as little as 10 minutes a day will have a great effect on your central nervous system and brain, reduce your stress, and enhance your well-being. No matter what age, Body Type, or mental, physical, or emotional status you present, meditation has no bad side effects and delivers the best high you can get. It's a GirlForce-boosting practice that will bring contentment, happiness, serenity, self-esteem, and confidence into your life.

Meditation Unleashes the
Full-Throttle Power of GirlForce

Meditation is the most direct way to contact GirlForce and establish its power within your body and mind. When you dive into meditation, you literally dive into your own internal paradise. You experience the universe in yourself and yourself in the universe. I know that's cosmic, but ride with me here for a second. Meditation is your key to spiritual insight, wisdom, and love. If you practice regularly, you'll discover that it's your link to good health, confidence, happiness, and peace.

There is no better way to hone your awareness than to meditate. The more you do it, the more you'll find the peaceful meditative state becomes established in your mind, body, and spirit.

OM Meditation Is for Everyone

The mantra, or sacred word, meditation is a snap. All you have to do is repeat a sacred word internally for 20 minutes, definitely once, but even better, twice a day. How easy is that?

Mantras vary according to the particular practice you follow, but of all the mantras, the most universal is "OM." This is the mantra used within the GirlForce Meditation Practice.

INSTRUCTIONS

* Sit in a comfortable, upright position, either sitting cross-legged on the floor or in a chair with a straight back that supports your spine. Close your eyes and listen to the sounds around you. Once you hear the sounds, recognize them and let them gently drift away, one by one, like clouds drifting through a clear, blue sky.
* Once you've let go of your awareness of the outside sounds, direct your focus inward and begin repeating the mantra OM internally. OM is pronounced "aum." (According to ancient Indian texts, OM is the mystical syllable that contains the sound that created the universe.) Simply allow the mantra to find its own natural rhythm. It does not have to synchronize with your breathing.
* Keep your eyes closed for 20 minutes, repeating the mantra. If your mind wanders—it will, especially when you're strung out—gently bring it back to the mantra. It's not a test to see how much you can stick to the mantra. Be gentle with yourself and allow the mantra to come and go naturally and effortlessly in your awareness. You may set a clock to ring after 20 minutes, but most people find they rouse themselves from meditation around this time.
* Keep your eyes closed and slowly begin to awaken your body, wriggling your toes and fingers, and bring your awareness back to your body and the room. Open your eyes gradually. Get up from your chair or sitting position slowly. It is best for the first few minutes after meditation not to expose yourself to any loud sounds, very bright light, strong odors, or strenuous activity.

As you can see from the above meditation instructions, there's nothing tricky about meditation. Even if you experience nothing but mind–chatter during meditation (planning the party next week, worrying about what your teacher will say about your latest essay, planning your shopping list), you are still meditating. A "good" meditation is one that you do!

You will discover when you meditate that as you repeat the mantra, it starts to come and go in your awareness, becoming more and more subtle. Where once it was a concrete thought in the form of a word, it soon becomes quite abstract, until it is left behind altogether and the mind becomes perfectly still.

If, during meditation, you become aware that you are thinking, falling asleep, or losing the mantra, the best thing to do is to go back to the pattern of repeating the mantra and gently continue with the practice.

Here are some helpful guidelines about how and where to meditate:

General Hints for the Practice of Meditation

- Breathe through your nose because nose breathing helps balance the vital energy in the body and keeps the mouth and respiratory system moist.
- The best times to practice are the early morning before breakfast when the body and mind are fresh and at sunset before dinner.
- Ideally your stomach should be empty when practicing meditation. Wait at least two hours after eating.
- Regularity is the key to receiving the full benefits of meditation. The body becomes habituated to the GirlForce-enhancing powers of meditation, and you'll discover that the more you practice it the more your body and mind will crave it.
- Meditate for as long as you can without straining. If 5 minutes is all you can manage, then that's good enough. Don't strain. Straining causes stress.

- Don't meditate for more than 20 minutes at each sitting. There are many advanced meditation practices that require longer sessions, but these practices should be guided by a trained meditation teacher.
- Meditation should be performed after, rather than before, any yoga postures.
- When you first start your practice of meditation, you may discover a few strange sensations such as light-headedness, tingling, heat or cold, extreme tiredness, or stomach gurgling. All these responses are perfectly normal by-products of releasing stress and toxins.
- Do not meditate outside or any place where you could be disturbed abruptly out of meditation. For example, it's not a good idea to meditate on the bus.

Start a GirlForce Experience Diary

List all your aims and objectives in a beautiful, lush diary. Then list all of your GirlForce-depleting habits (biting nails, eating too much junk food, complaining, gossiping about friends, and so on). Write down your feelings around these habits, like "gossiping keeps people away from me, gossiping makes me feel bad about myself," which will give you an insight into why you do something and why it is hard to quit.

Write down all the positive and negative things you experience as you start including GirlForce-boosting strategies in your life. When you look back at what you've written, say after six months, you will be surprised to see that the negative behaviors, habits, and addictions have effortlessly fallen away.

Anti-stress Affirmations

Like your meditation mantra, affirmations are a great fun way to practice boosting your self-esteem and confidence. Repeat them every day or get creative and make up your own. Some days you may feel like a fraud when you repeat "I am perfect just as I am," but affirmations work over time by retraining your mind to think positive thoughts about yourself. Sometimes it's a case of fake it till you make it. You'll be amazed at how good they make you feel!

Every day I feel the super-boosted confidence and power of GirlForce in me getting stronger.

I am perfect just as I am.

I'm a beautiful expression of nature. Each moment of my life is an opportunity to grow.

I am filled with bliss and completely open to change.

I am GirlForce.

I am always in contact with my spirit.

I am filled with love and kindness.

I am free from all cares, worries, and stress.

I live in the moment.

The Sacred Clearing Visualization

One great way to experience the benefits of Creative Visualization is to record your voice onto a CD reading out the Sacred Clearing Visualization on the opposite page. Play it back to yourself any time you feel stressed or in need of inspiration. Time the tape or CD to play 5 to 10 minutes.

Anti-stress Creative Visualization

Creative Visualization is a concentration technique used by many elite athletes and business people to help them perform at very high levels. Because the mind cannot distinguish between an actual event and an imagined event (the reason why you can get butterflies in the tummy with just the thought of speaking in public), Creative Visualization helps train the mind to think in positive ways. You can use Creative Visualization to train your mind to believe and trust in a successful outcome or increased health. Whatever it is that you desire you can use Creative Visualization to help you get it. And the more you visualize yourself as confident, healthy, powerful, strong, vital, serene, happy, or whatever it is that you'd like to be, you will build those qualities in yourself.

Like meditation, this visualization technique will send a surge of immune-boosting chemicals through your body, reducing stress and helping to establish peace and calm in the mind. It can be performed anytime you feel stressed out or imbalanced.

Close your eyes. Imagine you're walking through a heavily wooded forest. Even though there are many trees, you can see shafts of light filtering through the branches and the leaves. Very soon you notice a pathway leading to a clearing in the forest that is bathed in golden sunlight. The clearing has soft, fresh grass underfoot, and as you enter the clearing, you can smell the fresh grass and see the clear, blue sky above. As you stand in the clearing you are filled with wonder at the beauty of nature. After a few moments, you are taken by an impulse to sit on the grass. As you settle on the grass, you experience a growing sense of peace and serenity. You feel the warming sunlight falling all over your face and body. It is deeply nourishing and you become aware that the sunlight is mingled with another light—a bright, white, otherworldly light—that enters through the crown of your head and descends down your spine toward your bottom. This white light melts out from your spine and through your veins and finally floods every cell of your body. You are aware that this white light has beautiful qualities. It radiates compassion, kindness, love, and forgiveness, and it fills you with joy. Every fiber of your being is filled with joy as you sit on the grass in the clearing. After a few moments of soaking up the light, you become aware again of your body. You sense your feet and bottom resting on the grass, and you feel grounded yet energized. In time you awaken yourself from this bliss and get up from the grass. You are filled with confidence, energy, and vitality as you turn to face the path that leads you back into the forest. As you leave the clearing you are content in the knowledge that this sacred place is here for you whenever you need it. Whenever you want to retreat from the world to the beautiful, healing, sunlit clearing, all you need to do is close your eyes and you're there in an instant. As you stride through the forest, the path, trees, leaves, and foliage are dissolving while you come back to your body and the room. Once you are aware of the room, slowly open your eyes.

Be adventurous and write your own Creative Visualization. Set it at the beach or a party—anywhere you feel inspired and confident. See yourself climbing mountains, winning awards, or being an enlightened guru! Whatever makes you feel good.

Stress-Busting
Self-Pampering

1. Walk the dog. **2.** Save up and buy yourself a new outfit. **3.** Listen to your favorite song. **4.** Eat chocolate. **5.** Have an aromatherapy bath. **6.** Swap a massage with your best friend. **7.** Give yourself a manicure. **8.** Take a shower and lather yourself with a luxurious body product. **9.** Wear clothes that make you feel hot. **10.** Read a magazine. **11.** Plant some seeds and make yourself a herb pot. **12.** Pack a picnic and go to the beach or the park with your girlfriends. **13.** Take a stroll around the park and breathe the fresh air. **14.** Take an early morning swim in the ocean.

CHAPTER SEVEN

Get in Touch with Your Inner Self

GirlForce is a **party** you have all on your own. When you're **high** on **self-love** no one can bring you down. Supercharged with the power of **GirlForce**, YOU rock.

Want bulletproof self-esteem and mega-doses of confidence? Your Body Type is your key to understanding your emotions and feelings. Knowing what feelings your Body Type is likely to experience will help you handle all the emotional highs and lows of life. And when you learn stuff about all the different Types, you'll also discover lots of info about your parents and friends and the cute guys you crave.

DO YOU DREAM OF BEING MORE CONFIDENT? Maybe you want to be more popular? Perhaps you like yourself but you still criticize yourself every time you make a mistake. You'd be perfectly normal if you felt everyone but you is perfect and has everything together. But the truth is, most people feel less than fabulous a lot of the time. Low self-esteem is much more common than you'd suspect. And let's not get started about body image—most chicks go ballistic every time they have to try on a new bathing suit because they hate the sight of their butts in a bikini. And who doesn't stress about their skin?

Everyone gets down on themselves from time to time. What's NOT okay is hating yourself for every little thing you do wrong. What's NOT okay is beating yourself up if you don't like what you see in the mirror. *It's time to end the tyranny of low self-esteem and bust through the things that are holding you back from feeling totally hip, powerful, and cool.*

Let's start with what self-esteem really is. I know it's a buzzword, but you probably haven't really sat down to analyze what it means. Self-esteem is a psychological state that involves thinking, feeling, and behaving in ways that reflect an inner ability to *accept, respect, trust, and believe* in yourself.

When you *accept* yourself, you can live comfortably with both your personal strengths and weaknesses without excessive self-beatings. When you *respect* yourself, you acknowledge your own dignity and value yourself as a unique and worthwhile person. Having *trust* in yourself means that you have a deep and abiding belief in your ability to cope with life's ups and downs, and having *belief* in yourself means that you have the confidence to fulfill your wants, needs, hopes, and dreams.

No one can give you self-esteem. It doesn't come in a designer bag. It doesn't come from shedding pounds or getting rid of zits. It certainly isn't handed to you on a silver platter by the guy you kissed at last Saturday's party, and it doesn't come from being best friends with the most popular girl in school. Self-esteem is a quality that needs to come from within. And in most cases, it's a state that you need to develop—like a muscle that gets stronger when you exercise it, your self-esteem gets stronger if you work it!

Self-Esteem and GirlForce

It's no good telling people that they need to get self-esteem if you don't tell them where to look for it. One fast, no-nonsense way to cultivate self-esteem is to get in contact with the confidence-boosting power of your GirlForce, which lives in your very own heart and soul.

When you are in tune with your nature or your Body Type, you begin to accept yourself, and when that happens, GirlForce flows. Self-esteem and GirlForce go hand in hand. Self-esteem is the experience of self-love and self-acceptance. And self-acceptance is about being who you are—no conditions attached. Guess what? That's GirlForce!

How's Your Self-Esteem?

Are you the president of your own fan club or just a quiet member? Take this quiz to find out what kind of shape your self-esteem is in. I promise, no one will think you're full of yourself if you answer positively. And if your confidence is in the doldrums, you'll discover some cool ways to pick it up (later in this chapter and throughout the book).

Self-Esteem Quiz

1. How do you feel when you look in the mirror?

a) Where do I begin? There are thousands of things I'd like to change.

b) On the whole, I'm happy, but there are a couple of little things that could do with a bit of polishing.

c) I'm perfect just the way I am.

2. The most popular girl at school is throwing an end-of-the-year bash. Do you:

a) Put it out of your mind because you know you're too dull to be invited anyway.

b) Go shopping for a hot outfit, anticipating a fab time.

c) Walk straight up to her and ask her for your invite. You know no party is a success without you there.

3. Someone pays you a compliment. Do you:

a) Graciously say, "Thanks" and blush.

b) Say, "Yes, I know."

c) Believe it's a lie.

4. When I'm meeting new people I'm:

a) Extroverted—I'm generally the center of attention.

b) Shy and withdrawn.

c) Open but not in their faces.

5. The race is on for class president. Do you:

a) Campaign hard. You know you're perfect for the job.

b) Not give it a second's thought; no one would vote for you anyway.

c) Think it might be fun to have a shot at it; you never know what might happen if you give it a try.

6. Which animal do you most identify with?

a) Dolphin

b) Lion

c) Deer

7. When the teacher asks for those who know the answer to the math homework to raise their hands, and you know the right answer, do you:

a) Slink down in your seat. "I don't want anyone to look at me."
b) Put up your hand and wait patiently to be picked.
c) Call out, "I know the answer."

8. Getting dressed for a party, do you:

a) Go for something that will get lots of attention, maybe something flashy.
b) Go for the big cover up. My body sucks.
c) Just put on something I feel comfortable in.

9. If a hot guy asked you out, would you:

a) Think someone was playing a practical joke.
b) Be really flattered and look forward to getting to know him.
c) Check your calendar; "I get enough dates to pick and choose."

10. Which celebrity are you most like:

a) Blake Lively—I'm so hot I sizzle.
b) Sienna Miller—I'm a bit goofy, but I'm okay with my mistakes.
c) America Ferrera—I accept myself as I am.

Add Up Your Score

	a)	b)	c)
❶	a) 1	b) 2	c) 3
❷	a) 1	b) 2	c) 3
❸	a) 2	b) 3	c) 1
❹	a) 3	b) 1	c) 2
❺	a) 3	b) 1	c) 2
❻	a) 2	b) 3	c) 1
❼	a) 1	b) 2	c) 3
❽	a) 3	b) 1	c) 2
❾	a) 1	b) 2	c) 3
❿	a) 3	b) 1	c) 2

YOU NEED A SELF-ESTEEM INJECTION

Girlfriend, it's time to get with the game and stop giving yourself a hard time. Maybe you've had a rough time at home lately? Perhaps you're being bullied at school? Maybe you're not as gorgeous as Reese Witherspoon (so who is?). Whatever it is that's getting you down about yourself, it's time to give your self-esteem a kick and get on with living life. You have so much to offer the world (even if your talents are as yet undiscovered), and you have every right to be happy, confident, and cool.

Be proactive. Join a sporting club, do a yoga class, or even try doing some volunteer work—you'll discover helping others makes you feel good. Practice the affirmations you learned in Chapter Six. You'll see that in next to no time you'll feel better, and when you do, other people will pick up on your positive vibes and respond more positively to you. Beating yourself up is a complete waste of time and energy. Turn that negative self-talk into feel-good thinking.

IF YOU SCORED 15–25
YOU'RE OKAY WITH YOURSELF

You're pretty comfortable with who you are. You're good in a crowd and, while you don't necessarily crave the limelight, you're confident about your friendships. No one would accuse you of being full of yourself. At the same time, you could do with a little more oomph when it comes to putting yourself forward. Take advantage of the situation the next time you're in a position to shine. When you look in the mirror, you like what you see. You know you're not Miss Universe, but with a little lip gloss and a smile you know you can light up a room. Having balance means you're able to cope with life's peaks and troughs. Sometimes it's good to take a risk and maybe even fail—trust that your self-esteem can take whatever blows life hands out. Keep up the good work.

IF YOU SCORED 25–30
YOU'RE SUPER CONFIDENT

Your self-esteem is practically off the register. You're so confident you positively ooze charm. You're in the fantastic position of feeling terrific about yourself. You know life can be tough at times, but it's not going to knock you down. Superpowered self-esteem is a gift. It's really important though to realize that not everyone is endowed with the same high-voltage glamour and sex appeal as you, and remember to be compassionate with your girlfriends who don't feel as fab about themselves as you do. When you check yourself out in the mirror, you see perfection looking back at you, which is great. But also remember beauty is only skin-deep, and it's what you've got on the inside that really counts.

Your Body Type Is a Key to Self-Esteem and Self-Acceptance

When the media constantly throws up images of so-called perfection—models, celebrities, athletes—it's no wonder we feel it's tough to accept ourselves. Advertisements, movies, magazines, and TV shows all tell us there is only one way to be—famous, thin, fit, beautiful, confident, and in control. That sucks big-time.

This very limited view of what a "successful" person is all about leads to bad feelings of self-hatred, self-disgust, low self-worth, and low self-esteem. Of course the media is not solely to blame; we also have racism, prejudice, societal pressures, and fear to thank for our lack of self-esteem.

But you don't have to succumb to the pressure to look and be a certain way. There's another path you can take: the GirlForce path, which shows you that it's not only okay to be yourself, it's positively cool to love yourself.

The first step to developing self-esteem is self-acceptance. Self-acceptance means allowing yourself to be exactly WHO YOU ARE without having to make any changes. GirlForce is about helping you make changes to your lifestyle to improve your health and well-being, but one of its primary goals is to help you accept who you are, before you embark on the sometimes challenging path of change.

The wisdom and know-how you got from learning about your particular Body Type is in itself a path to self-acceptance. When you accept the strengths and limitations of your individual body and mind, you build self-esteem. When you stop comparing yourself to others, you build self-esteem. When you learn to enjoy your kooky quirks and idiosyncrasies instead of judging them, you build self-esteem. Your Body Type is your passport to self-acceptance, self-esteem, and GirlForce.

One thing to keep in mind is that self-esteem does not develop overnight and is rarely the result of a single blinding insight. Self-esteem is built gradually through your willpower to work on your mind, body, and spirit.

Discover Your Emotional Side

By now you're probably getting the hang of how different Body Types manifest different physical traits. Fire girls are often strong and athletic, Air girls are thinner and more nimble, and Earth girls are curvier and more relaxed than other girls. But the physical traits are only part of the

One fast,
no-nonsense way
to cultivate self-esteem
is to get in contact with
the confidence-boosting
power of your GirlForce,
which lives in your very
own heart and soul.

picture. Mind powers and emotions are also expressed differently through the different elemental-energies Air, Fire, and Earth.

For example, Fire vixens manifest fiery emotions such as passion, optimism, and hot-headedness while Air chicks manifest airy emotions such as flightiness, creativity, and enthusiasm. Earth babes tend to be earthy, relaxed, grounded, and dreamy. When you accept the wild and wonderful traits of your particular Body Type, you have taken a huge step toward self-acceptance and self-esteem.

It's cool to discover that many of our personality traits, as well as our physical traits, are built into our systems at birth. Which is not to say that we don't have to take responsibility for them or discover ways to master them, but it does mean that many of our vulnerabilities and weaknesses are inherited traits that represent no failing on our part.

When we know that we are predisposed to certain psychological traits, we open the path to self-acceptance, self-esteem, and self-love. There's no point struggling against yourself. If you are predisposed to anxiety and nervousness, the best thing you can do is to accept it. Then, take positive steps toward minimizing any potential harm that your nervous and anxious temperament can exact on your body, mind, and spirit.

Your Body Type holds the key to self-understanding, self-acceptance, and self-respect, and finally, self-mastery.

The Personality Profiles

One thing to know from the start, there is no "right" and "wrong" when it comes to our personalities. The elemental-energies Air, Fire, and Earth are metaphors for physical and psychological states. Just like your star sign, they represent a "zodiac" of tendencies and archetypes. They work as focal points directing your attention to parts of yourself that you may not have considered. The idea here is to get to know yourself better, not to become fixed about the things that are right or wrong in the Profile and not to be judgmental about yourself or others.

The Personality Profiles are designed to shed light on parts of your personality that are sometimes elusive. It's unlikely that you will read all the information and agree with every point (remember we all have Air, Fire, and Earth within us). You may find that you identify with a lot of the Profile, and in identifying yourself and your traits, you discover a new and deeper understanding of yourself and your motivations.

The Air Personality Profile

THE SENSITIVE AIR GIRL feels she is running in a different race from the high-achieving Fire and cruising Earth girls in her group.

Air girls are natural rebels and often enjoy the role of the interesting outsider. They are inventive, quick-witted, and creative thinkers. They make wonderful teachers, inspired philosophers and lecturers, gifted musicians, tireless charity organizers, clever bankers, and because of their acute sense of justice for all, wise diplomats and fierce freedom fighters. They are often found behind the scenes of a hard-fought social or political battle and provide the strategy for many a crusade.

In a family situation, Air girls often play out the role of the sensitive one who feels emotional, mental, and spiritual pain deeply. Writing poetry, keeping a journal, or songwriting are ways Air girls like to express their feelings. They are likely to be compassionate, understanding, and unconditionally accepting of others.

While a consistent daily schedule is important for Air Types, they can often feel stifled by routine, which may threaten to strangle the creative energy essential for the well-being of the Air girl. The trick is to find a balance between a health-giving routine and a more spontaneous existence. It's not a good idea for any of the Types to abuse their bodies with drugs or alcohol, but the Air girl's delicate system is not made for trashing.

The Air Type is capable of passionate and deep love and also has the gift of experiencing love on a spiritual level. Many Air girls can freak out their parents with their early interest in romantic relationships.

Of all the Types, the Air personality is probably the most misunderstood. In the modern world, where we make ready judgments of others, Air girls can appear kooky and eccentric. To cast them in a mold and dismiss them as strange is to miss out on the richness and depth of this fascinating Type. Their insights can teach the rest of us how to release pent-up emotions. As natural-born rebels, they allow us all the freedom to break rules—an important part of becoming self-aware. The Air girl's energy is creative, spiritually aware, eccentric, adventurous, intellectual, freewheeling, and exciting. The Air elemental-energy can be extremely challenging because it constantly craves change. (Are you driving your parents and friends nuts because you often fantasize about overseas travel and exotic adventures?) This delicate, sensitive, and aware girl reveals the grace, power, and innovation found in the human spirit.

The Fire Personality Profile

THE FIRE GIRL IS FORGED THROUGH the heat of her passions. No other Type is more ferociously determined than the Fire warrior woman. She is rarely denied anything she wants, because she's prepared to stop at nothing to get it. The upside of this trait is that she can be a tireless campaigner who remains optimistic and energetic even in the face of adversity. The downside is that she can be bossy, overbearing, and prone to the odd hissy fit.

Unlike Air types, who can deal with austerity, it's common for dynamic Fire girls to be seduced by their desires—they not only crave food and attention, they also lust after the latest fab shoes, jewelry, and makeup. Their strong desire for leadership often takes them to the giddy heights of stardom. Because they have a natural flare for achievement (think Nicole Kidman), burnout is a risk for Fire girls who have not learned how to temper their flaming desires.

Fire gals are pioneers. They are often found in the halls of power, and they're commonly the CEOs of big corporations, the architects of monumental schemes, Academy Award winners, the sportswomen who become heroines, and the visionaries who see the end goal when the picture looks gloomy.

The Fire elemental-energy is innately active, so the more passive energies (Earth and Air), can be difficult for Fire personalities to understand. Patience, compassion, and consideration for others are not Fire girls' strong suits. However, they benefit massively when they can cultivate these qualities in themselves, learning how to nurture themselves and others.

In a family situation, Fire girls are usually cast in the role of the archetypal warrior. They are lovers *and* fighters. They are fearless and sometimes arrogant about their abilities, and their acute intelligence helps them to win many arguments. (If you've been giving your parents a hard time and always trying to get your own way, it might be good to take the heat off them once in a while.) That said, Fire girls are incredibly independent, fiercely loyal, devoted, and loving—awesome traits, which most parents value.

Fire babes make exciting friends and girlfriends. Their willingness to take on a challenge is a total turn-on. Whether they're on the shy side or "out there" extroverts, the thing you most notice about Fire babes is their intensity. Fire Types are true princesses, and they make benevolent rulers. We learn strength, passion, honor, courage, and leadership from the Fire elemental-energy—qualities that are essential for all of us.

Fire

The Earth Personality Profile

NOTICED THAT YOUR FRIENDS spill their secrets to you? Are you the one to settle an argument? Grounded, stable, nurturing, and loving, the Earth girl is the natural Earth Mother who always knows the right things to say.

Compared to the serene and laid-back Earth angels, the flightiness of Air and the fiery ambition of Fire seem like big contrasts. On a metaphorical level, Earth Types are made of the water and earth elemental-energies, the stuff that makes up most of the surface of the planet. For this reason, Earth Types are incredibly connected to nature and also quite attached to earthly existence and the material world. Earth girls can get into trouble when their attachments to the world become excessive and they overindulge their senses and hunger for material possessions. (Hankered for a handbag lately? Desired a designer label dress recently?) One of the most worthwhile spiritual practices Earth girls can do is clean out their closets and give their old stuff away to charity.

In the family context, Earth girls are not the rebels that their Air siblings or friends might be or the warriors that their Fiery gal pals are. They're not too good to be true, but they don't like arguments and tend to be the peacemakers in the family. They are devoted and loving daughters, but it's also important for Earth girls to realize that sometimes it's good to break out and go wild. (That doesn't mean stealing the car, trashing yourself, and staying out till dawn, it just means taking risks from time to time.)

Of all the Types, Earth girls are the most sensuous. They appreciate the finer things in life and love food, art, fine clothes, and beauty. Despite society's obsession with the idea that beauty equates to thinness, Earth girls are often surprised to find they are as attractive to the opposite sex as their Air and Fire sisters.

Earth girls are at their best when they are stimulated. If they're bored or undervalued they can become lethargic and stubborn. They have a tendency to become introverted and self-sabotaging without routine, so they do well when there is structure and discipline. Earth girls are natural artists, healers, and chefs. You'll often find Earth Types in the arts, and they have an ability to combine their earthy, practical skills with a refined sense of beauty and magic. Poetry, music, dance, medicine, psychology, interior design, and the visual arts capture the true refinement of these girls. We learn nurturing, compassion, endurance, and love of beauty from the Earth elemental-energy.

The Personality Traits of Air, Fire, and Earth

When you can objectively recognize your qualities (and your personal trouble spots), you begin to see yourself as others do. Check out these traits and see how many you can identify in yourself.

We all have positive and negative traits in our personalities. The trick for all of us is to become aware of both sides of our personalities and work with them. The idea is not to judge ourselves but to recognize the light and dark sides of ourselves and be clear when either side is operating. That's called being responsible for our stuff.

FIRE GIRLS often exhibit the following traits: passionate, committed, intelligent, noble, courageous, powerful, self-confident, honorable, loyal, secure, robust, clear-thinking, exacting, wise, perceptive, intense, funny, playful, glamorous, good instincts, cooperative, and active. PERSONALITY TRAITS for the Fire girl to work on: perfectionist, arrogant, proud, competitive, judgmental, aggressive, critical, extremist, and controlling.

AIR GIRLS often exhibit the following traits: exciting, hopeful, perceptive, understanding of others, thinks a lot, witty, acute intellect, spiritually aware, enthusiastic, adventurous, creative, open-minded, sensitive, light-hearted, innovative, soulful, fascinating, and curious. PERSONALITY TRAITS for the Air girl to work on: restless, poor body image, feelings of isolation, flighty, insecure, and poor long-term memory.

EARTH GIRLS often exhibit the following traits: loving, compassionate, nurturing, inclusive, kind, serene, graceful, mysterious, stable, sensual, artistic, dreamy, devoted, grounded, tolerant, seductive, reliable, good sense of humor, easygoing, capable, likable, and friendly. PERSONALITY TRAITS for the Earth girl to work on: sometimes lethargic, lazy, slow-moving, possessive, unmovable, procrastination, protective, sullen, withdrawn, and greedy.

My Issues

If you scored between 10–15 on the Self-Esteem Test, it's possible
that you have some tough issues in your life that you're trying to work
through. Here are some of the circumstances psychologists say lead to low
self-esteem. Don't be afraid to talk to your doctor or school counselor or
seek the advice of a professional psychologist if you can identify any of
these issues impacting on how you feel about yourself.

1. **Overly critical parents:** Do your parents give you a hard time about
your grades, your appearance, or your choice of music or friends? If so
you need to find ways to compromise with them. Discuss with them
how it makes you feel when they criticize you. Try this script as a
starting point: "*When you* criticize me *it makes me feel* bad about
myself. *I need* you to cut me some slack by allowing me to express
myself. This would help me a lot. Thanks for listening." If your parents
have different cultural beliefs, it might make it easier for you to write
things down in a respectful note expressing how you feel and why
their behavior seems harsh and strict to you. I know this is hard, but it
will open the channels to mature negotiation with your parents.

2. **Physical abuse by parents and/or authority figures:** Have you
ever been physically hurt by your parents or some older person, such as
a teacher? Have you ever been sexually abused? If this has happened, or
is happening to you, you need some professional help immediately. Go
to a trusted parent, a teacher, the school counselor, or your family
doctor to discuss the issues. If you are being physically or sexually
abused and cannot trust an adult in your close circle, call the National
Child Abuse Hotline at 1-800-4-A-CHILD or the National Sexual
Assault Hotline at 1-800-656-HOPE. You can also find their Web sites
at www.childhelp.org and www.rainn.org. It will take courage and it
may be scary to tell the counselor or social worker about your
situation, but this is a starting point for healing and dealing.

3. **Abandonment by parents or caregivers:** Are your parents still
together? If mom or dad left you at an early age, it could be impacting
your self-esteem. Family breakdown is tough territory and very
common. At least one in five families is affected by the breakdown of
parental relationships. Even if you still have a relationship with the
parent who left the home, you can have persistent feelings that he or
she abandoned you, which may make you feel depressed and down on
yourself. Keep a journal of your thoughts and feelings about this

issue and if you need extra help, seek out someone to talk to: a school counselor or your family doctor. You don't have to tough it out.

4. **Loss of a parent early in life:** Losing a parent is tough at any age, let alone when you're young. This loss may be causing you to feel abandoned and depressed. People can be sad about the loss of their parents for many years after the event. Talk about the issues with a trusted friend or counselor. Be real about how much the loss of your parent affected you and your family—emotionally, spiritually, and financially. It's hard to handle the fact that they won't be around to see you grow up or show up at your school concerts. Talk to your surviving parent (if you have one) or a trusted adult about your sadness, or if you need to, ask them to help you to seek the advice of a grief counselor.

5. **Parental drug or alcohol abuse:** This is another area where it's vital to get professional help. There is nothing to be ashamed of—it's not your fault that your mom or dad or siblings are using drugs or alcohol to cope with life; drug or alcohol addiction is a disease and can be treated. Here are some things you need to do to help YOU cope. Call the National Drug and Alcohol Treatment Referral Routing Service at 1-800-662-HELP to talk to someone and/or find a local organization where you can get help. Ask for someone who can discuss drug abuse in the family and what services are available to help you cope. Visit your family doctor and let him or her know what's going on at home. It's not betraying your mom or dad; it's a way to make sure you, your siblings, and your mom or dad are protected if there's an emergency. Make sure you have emergency numbers for a doctor at hand. Keep a diary of the events. Hopefully, one day you'll be able to share that with your parents. Whatever you do, don't go through it alone.

6. **Parental neglect or rejection:** There's a difference between not getting on with your parents and your parents leaving you for days, weeks, or months to fend for yourself. Maybe they can't or won't look after themselves or you. In this situation, you need help. Call 1-800-4-A-CHILD to report that you have been left alone or neglected.

7. **Parental overprotectiveness:** We're not talking about your mom and dad worrying about you going to a concert or getting your nose pierced (all parents worry about this stuff); this is about them not trusting you to make any of your own decisions and undermining your choices of friends, school subjects, clothes, etc. Here's a situation where you need to hone your negotiation skills and build their trust over time. Perhaps try this: "I know you're uncomfortable about my choices

for myself, but I want to assure you that you can trust me. I am aware of the risks of my choices (by giving up math I'll never be a scientist like Dad, or by hanging out with Sarah and her friends you're worried that I'll get into the wrong crowd) but I need some space to make my own mistakes and learn from them. Okay?" By preempting the things that they will be freaking out about, you'll show them that you understand their concerns.

Some additional contacts

BOYS TOWN
Don't be fooled by the name, it's not just for boys! Call 24 hours a day with any issue, including suicide, depression, school troubles, abuse, etc.
1-800-448-3000
www.boystown.org

NATIONAL DOMESTIC VIOLENCE HOTLINE
1-800-799-SAFE
www.ndvh.org

NATIONAL TEEN DATING ABUSE HELPLINE
1-866-331-9474
www.loveisrespect.org

NATIONAL YOUTH CRISIS HOTLINE
1-800-442-HOPE

NATIONAL RUNAWAY SWITCHBOARD
Call if you are thinking about running away from home, have a friend who has run and you're looking for help, or you are a runaway ready to go home.
1-800-RUNAWAY
ww.1800runaway.org

COVENANT HOUSE NINELINE
Call to talk about your concerns. Anywhere. Anytime.
1-800-999-9999
www.covenanthouse.org

THERE ARE LOTS OF LOCAL PLACES YOU CAN GO FOR HELP TOO!
- Your local church, temple, or place of worship
- Your local Red Cross
- Your doctor or the school nurse
- Your school guidance counselor or a trusted teacher or coach
- A friend's mom or dad
- Any adult you trust

Plug into the Joy Within—
It's Easier Than You Think

Ahhhh, a full tank of self-esteem. Can't you just picture it? Going to parties feeling completely confident (even when not everyone there likes you), talking to hot guys without turning into jelly, trying on cute clothes without gagging or worrying that you're not going to look like Cameron Diaz. Sound like heaven?

Well, guess what, now you know the secret to feeling totally cool, calm, and confident! GirlForce is your secret weapon in the charge for bulletproof self-esteem. GirlForce gives you kick-ass confidence. You know deep down that you're okay exactly as you are. And the more you work with your body and emotions, and the more aware of your qualities and quirks you become, the more you'll get hip to its powers. Right now there's nothing standing between you and self-esteem. Are you ready to unleash the superstar within?

CHAPTER EIGHT

Talking about Relationships

Wanna create good karma every day? Thanks to **GirlForce** you have the key to dreamy relationships. **Girl power** helps you deal with your own stuff and gives you **wisdom** and **compassion** to be totally loving. Discover how to be the best person you can be.

Why do you find one girl in your group a complete bore while another girl is heaven to be with? Body Types go a long way to answering why you pick some people to be your best friends and freak about the rest. Check out how the different Body Types get along with each other, and while you're at it, find out how to pick the perfect guy, how to be a better friend, and how to deal with pesky siblings. Once you've worked out the secrets to being a cool and together person, you'll be a total inspiration to everyone around you. Bring it on!

MAYBE YOU'RE ALREADY CLUED IN on the ins and outs of relationships. Maybe you're one of those angels who always gets along with everyone. If you never fight with your parents, never have disagreements with your friends, never have problems with your brothers and sisters or crises with your crush, then you don't need to read on. If you're like most people, who find relationships a bit baffling at times, then you're about to open a treasure chest of info and know-how that will help you navigate a path to relationship heaven. (Well, maybe not heaven, but a place within yourself where you feel you have all the tools and techniques you need to make the relationships in your life work.)

You could be the coolest girl in the world with a million wannabes trying to be your friend, but it would all be hollow if you didn't know how to treat other people. Everything revolves around relationships. If you can't get along with people, the world becomes a small, miserable place. It's essential to understand that being happy isn't always about getting what you want. It's also about being kind, compassionate, and loving.

The best way to make sure your relationships remain happy, harmonious, and loving is to work on yourself. *That means taking responsibility for the things in your life that stress you out and the parts of yourself that freak you out.* In this way you become spiritually aware, which is the understanding that you and your emotions play a part in the great web of life and is a huge key to building relationships. When we understand that we are all part of something—our families, our communities, our nations, the whole human race—we realize that relationships form the basis of every creative and constructive thing humans do, but also every destructive thing we do, such as war and genocide. Good relationships are aware relationships, and it all starts with you and your attitudes.

Relationships are an awesome mirror of how you view yourself. You will often be attracted to people who have qualities that you like in yourself and often be grossed out by those who exhibit the tendencies that you hate and wish to disown in yourself. If you can embrace all people, the ones who make you feel comfortable as well as the ones who make you feel uncomfortable, you will become a whole lot wiser, kinder, and more compassionate, and you'll discover that you will feel more at ease with yourself. (Just think about it. It doesn't feel good pouring a lot of negative energy in someone's direction; they feel your negativity toward them, but you also feel the horrible sensations of judgment, jealousy, and criticism within you.)

When you see that other people suffer all the same stresses and challenges—not doing well in class, not feeling pretty enough, illness, relationship problems, family distress, loneliness, isolation, prejudice, and sadness—you will see that you are part of a huge family of human beings. *Compassion is the natural expression of the understanding that, despite our differences, we are all alike.* GirlForce flows through you like a ray of sunshine when you allow compassion, kindness, and love to fill your body, mind, and spirit.

And if you go further, and you actually put yourself out there and take steps to help someone else, you'll not only bring them happiness, you'll also spread GirlForce. GirlForce is an inexhaustible wellspring of love that, when shared between people, spills out and overflows into the family, the community, the planet, and the universe. Go, girl, be a force for good and share the girl power within!

One of the main reasons for using the GirlForce philosophy is to connect you to the cool, sassy, sweet, and loving part of yourself—your GirlForce.

How Different Body Types Behave in Relationships

The knowledge of how your Body Type affects your health and well-being is precious and can help you with every aspect of your life, including your relationships. It offers you greater self-understanding, why you act and react the way you do, and it increases your understanding of why the people you love and connect with act and react the way they do.

The knowledge of how different Body Types act and react is really handy when it comes to figuring people out. When you know your best friend is a Fire babe, you'll know this about her: she's passionate, she's committed, she's focused, and she's a go-getter. When you know your mom is an Air Type and prone to getting nervous and anxious about stuff, you can find ways to help her calm down, like making her a cup of tea and giving her a head massage. Or if you know the hottie you want is a slow and steady Earth guy, you'll know that the best way to get his attention is not to be in his face and rush him but to woo him with romantic gestures.

It's much easier to understand people who share the same Body Type as you. But the world would be a pretty boring place if we were all the same Type. According to Ayurveda, partnerships made of the same Type make for easy and harmonious connections while those made up of different Types make for exciting, growthful, and stimulating relationships.

Just remember that as we're all made up of all three elemental-energies—Air, Fire, and Earth—you may see aspects of your personality in the ways all three Types behave in relationships.

Air in Relationships

Air girls and guys are vivacious, communicative, demonstrative, and adventurous. Of all the Body Types, they are the most sensitive and need lots of encouragement and positive feedback. Their eccentricities make them a little outside the norm so they usually attract like-minded people who get a buzz out of their individuality and cute and funny ways.

Air chicks and guys are often witty, entertaining, creative, inspiring, fair-minded, rebellious, challenging, and innovative. When they're stressed they can be anxious, insecure, frightened, demanding, nervous, and neurotic. When they're out of balance, they need nurturing, kindness, gentleness, and compassion. They make devoted, although sometimes inconsistent, boyfriends or girlfriends—when they're on, they're on, when they're off, they're off. They are often the most interested in romantic relationships of all the Types, and when they are in a committed relationship they are capable of deep passion, which can be truly yummy. Their perceptiveness can blow you away and their gentle sensitivities can inspire true romance.

Him: He's energetic, optimistic, and motivated, although sometimes scattered and erratic. He's cheeky, the sweet-natured troublemaker who can't resist walking on the wild side. His spontaneity and inventiveness surprise and delight everyone and his quirky ways are gorgeously charismatic. The Air guy is impulsive and predictably unpredictable. He has a natural aversion to authority. So if you want to tame him, you'll have to do it without trying to rope him in. Calm him with sweet words and encouragement because behind the bravado he's a sensitive guy without a killer ego. If you have a tiff he'll disappear like a puff of smoke, so go easy on him and give him space to do his own thing.

Her: She's a believer in truth, justice, and the GirlForce way. She's probably the most spiritually aware of all the Types, and she loves writing poetry and songs, which reveal her deepest insights. She's always talking, so get ready to put her number on redial in your phone; she can literally have all-night chat-fests that leave you exhausted and her buzzing. She's your most eccentric friend. She's easily wounded, and she takes what you say to heart. Be careful not to offend her because she's not as thick-skinned as Fire or Earth Types. You love her because she's a true original.

Fire in Relationships

Fire vixens and warriors are passionate and romantic when they fall in love. They make committed partners and focused boyfriends and girlfriends who take their relationships very seriously. Their decisiveness and ambition make them attractive as team players, but beware: Fire Types like to lead and you may find they've taken over the project or the relationship.

When they're in balance, Fire guys and gals are loyal, big-hearted, generous, compassionate, and energetic. When they're out of balance, they can be aggressive, egotistical, insensitive, cruel, impatient, and selfish. Fire Types make wonderful girlfriends and boyfriends if you're secure in yourself, but they can get frustrated if they feel their partners are not up to their speed. At their best, Fire Types are the archetypal warriors who will stop at nothing to protect their loved ones. If their energy and strength are properly channeled, Fire Types make powerful and stimulating girlfriends and boyfriends. When they're out of balance, they need calm, soothing, and gentle nurturing to turn down the heat. Try not to fight fire with fire.

Him: The fiery energy of this guy is enough to blow your socks off. He's charismatic and courageous, and he settles for nothing but the best. He never does things by halves; he likes a challenge and has no problem with asserting himself. If you want to catch a Fire guy, you'll need to charm him with your confidence. His "take no prisoners" approach to life is not for the faint-hearted, so be bold and brazen and show him that you're every bit the passionate chick. He can also be attracted by intelligence and mystery, so you don't have to give everything away on the first date. Remember that Fire Types can burn out. He also needs time out to relax and unwind. Plan downtime where you can simply chill and have fun—a great way to open his big heart.

Her: She's the cheerleader type who can't resist a challenge. At times she appears arrogant and self-righteous, but assertion is one of her greatest assets and she manages to charm most people with the flick of her hair or a pout. Her pioneering spirit is one thing, but she's also blessed with courage, which is why she's usually the one who initiates change and paves the way for others—whether it's inventing a new hairstyle or insisting you all get your legs waxed together. She's loyal, she's passionate, she's clever, and she's the kind of friend you need in a crisis (if she can take her mind off the other million things that are absorbing her). She's great at getting things done and she throws a fab party. You'll thrive as her friend if you understand that she's on a mission and you can help her get there.

Earth in Relationships

Earth guys and girls are steady, calm, easygoing, affectionate, and loving. They make caring, sweet, generous friends and devoted boyfriends and girlfriends. Earth Types are said to be the most sensuous of all the Types and are affectionate and cuddly. They're overtly kind, artistic, and compassionate when they're in balance and lazy, possessive, and withdrawn when they are out of balance.

Earth Types are natural entertainers and throw lavish parties and celebrations. When they are stimulated in a relationship they are open, generous, and friendly. When they are ignored or treated insincerely, they become depressed and lackluster. Earth Types need challenge and change to remain at their peak, so boredom or excessive routine is not necessarily a great motivator for them. They respond well to beauty and appreciation, so when they receive those two things they thrive. When Earth Types slip out of balance, they need to be stimulated and excited with new and challenging ideas and proposals. Keep down-to-earth guys and laid-back girls excited with exotic adventures.

Him: He's blessed with natural poise and charm. He's cool, calm, and collected and sometimes hard to read. He's Mr. Maturity and his sophisticated tastes can be highly attractive to girls. He can be a bit conservative and his "think before he acts" approach can sometimes seem a bit stuffy. Considerate of other people's feelings, the Earth guy likes being good and doing good. He's a stickler for detail and he notices when you change your hair. He has modesty, intelligence, and style, and if you want to be his pal, the best approach is to be yourself; he'll appreciate the lack of pretentiousness. If he's down or out of whack, he'll be lazy, boring, and withdrawn. He's at his sparkling best when he's stimulated and excited. A rut is hell for the Earth guy, so make sure you never get into a slow groove. His dreamy side is romantic and sweet, and it's tempered with respect and affection.

Her: She hates wasting energy, loathes being rushed, and although it can take her longer to get motivated, once she's on a roll she's unstoppable. Mellower than most, her cool way of asserting herself gets your admiration and respect. She's not the most up-front girl and can be shy about approaching guys, but her soft, gentle, feminine ways are sweet and magnetic. Blessed with patience and stability, she's often the counselor of your group. Her grounded energy gives her the discipline to save for a new wardrobe but can also make her a little set in her ways. If you think she needs a style injection, don't overwhelm her with fast changes; take her shopping and gently encourage her to let go of those old jeans that are so yesterday. She's a kind and committed friend who will love you for life. Go ahead, bask in her gentle but firm friendship.

let's get to- gether

When you cultivate respect, love, and compassion for all the people in your life, your relationships bloom like a perfect flower.

Air and Air

Since Air people are the most eccentric and individualistic of all the Types, they make mesmerizing, magnetic, and invigorating partners. They thrive on the understanding that someone of the same Type can offer. They love to talk, connect, think up grand schemes, go dancing, and invent new dress styles. Air and Air together is an ideal union. They are Romeo and Juliet, the misunderstood young runaways who will change the world—if they only had five bucks for a bus ride out of town. When Air Types get together they often feel that they've found their soul mates; however, they're also in danger of turning fun and excitement into chaos— they go to bed late, talk too long and too much, allow mess to accumulate, and forget about food and exercise. Without daily rituals and routines, a relationship between two Air people can become dysfunctional, erratic, and eventually destructive. If Air partners can be disciplined enough to introduce routine into their daily lives (like eating regularly, taking long walks together, getting plenty of rest), they can maintain successful, creative, stimulating, and adventurous relationships.

Fire and Fire

Two Fire Types in a relationship is a potent and powerful combination. Each will allow the other the full expression of his or her ambition and talents. They will be the ultimate power couple, a stimulating pair that will be able to accomplish much in the way of material and financial success. Fire and Fire are an active couple. You'll often find them doing outdoorsy stuff together on the weekend, setting new challenges, and soaring to new heights. They like to hang out in a group, and they're often the glamour couple that everyone admires. The Fire Types' need to be right about everything can get in the way of a harmonious partnership. Arguments erupt when both stand their ground and refuse to back off. If each of the pair is prepared to compromise and let go of being right some of the time, the partnership will work. If neither will relinquish control and continue to fight for the position of power, the relationship will, over time, crumble and disintegrate. Compromise is the key to making Fire partnerships work.

Earth and Earth

When you put two laid-back partners together you get a happy, harmonious, and affectionate couple. This pair loves nothing better than to hang, watch TV, chat, and eat yummy food. They're cozy together. They don't crave much attention outside the relationship, so Earth and Earth surprise everyone with their ability to just be together and seemingly do very little. The danger facing two Earth Types is that they can slide into lethargy and laziness, watch too much TV, eat too much junk, and allow bad habits to take over the partnership. The natural tendency of Earth is to go toward slowness and sluggishness, so both people in an Earth and Earth relationship must ensure that they remain active, disciplined, and stimulated. Exercise and a program of challenge and change must be introduced into this partnership. Adventure and an active social life will help this pair stay happy and healthy together.

Air and Fire

Air and Fire make fascinating partners. The freewheeling and flighty Air Type gives light relief to the serious and organized Fire Type. They are intellectually stimulated by each other and can spend hours talking and debating subjects they are passionate about. The caution for this couple is that unless the Fire Type is sensitive to the Air Type's needs, the relationship can dissolve into arguments and upsets. The fragile Air Type needs reassurance and kindness, which can be challenging for impatient Fire Types. Fire Types can also be prone to jealousy, which can stifle the adventurous Air Type. In this instance, Air Types may need to curb their need to share themselves around too much and concentrate on their partner's needs first. Fire Types must also give the spacious Air personality lots of room to grow.

Air and Earth

Earth's steadiness can provide a terrific anchor for the erratic Air Type, and the Air Type can provide the much needed challenge and stimulation for Earth. As a couple, these two appear to be night and day—one earthy and grounded and the other airy and flighty, but as boyfriends and girlfriends they make sweet music together. The union between these Types can be loving and sensitive, as both like to delve into the subtle areas of the mind and spirit. As a pair, these two will love to surround themselves with beauty. The problem area for an Air and Earth partnership is that the Air person can find the Earth person too stuffy and old-fashioned while the Earth person can become a bit judgmental about the Air person's eccentricities. If both people in the partnership can just allow the other to be who they are, the relationship can be strong and long-lasting.

Fire and Earth

The Earth Type's cool steadiness makes a good foil for the Fire's hotheadedness and competitiveness. Earth Types don't tend to take Fire's impatience or selfishness as personally as Air Types, so this combination can be enduring and harmonious. Fire Types can become annoyed at Earth's slowness, but if the Fire person can learn to cool down and go slow, and the Earth person can pick up the pace a little, they'll discover the joys of their relationship. As romantic partners, this combination is very successful. Fire benefits from the sensuousness of Earth, and Earth benefits from the vigor of Fire. If both partners make an effort to be tolerant and openhearted, this combination can have a fun, challenging, and loving relationship.

Make Your Relationships Work Better

Stress is the single biggest threat to happy, harmonious relationships. When we're stressed we dump our fears, insecurities, and tensions on the people around us. If you want to get along with people—your friends, your parents, your siblings, and your crush—you gotta clean up your act. That means taking responsibility for your moods and feelings and learning how to deal with them.

Living in tune with your Body Type will go a long way to eliminating stress in your life. But you also have to handle your moods and emotions if you want stress-free relationships.

There are a few key qualities you need to cultivate in yourself every day if you want happy and together relationships:

Love

is probably the most overused word in the English language. We say we love pizza or we love that new lip gloss, but love is much more than attachment to things or experiences—it's actually devotion. The highest form of love in life is the love and devotion we share between friends, families, and communities. Love is something we often take for granted, but it's actually a quality that needs cultivating, like a plant that you lovingly tend as it buds and flowers. It's essential to let the love within you flow like a river. Let it pour over the people you care for. Don't be stingy with love; it will only make you feel small. Let the love within you grow so big that it overflows into the world.

Respect

means valuing each other's points of view. It means being open to being wrong. It means accepting people as they are. It means not dumping on someone because you're having a bad day. It means being polite and kind—always—because being kind to people is not negotiable. It means not dissing people because they're different from you. It means not gossiping about people or spreading lies or rumors. Being respectful is cool because consideration for others gives you a connection to GirlForce.

Compassion

is an internal state of mind where you make an effort to empathize with other people and put yourself in their shoes. It involves asking yourself, "I wonder how she feels about her parents getting divorced? I wonder how he feels when he's being bullied?" Compassion is a feeling of caring for other people's well-being. In the Buddhist sense, compassion can be roughly defined in terms of a state of mind that is nonviolent, nonharming, and nonaggressive. It is a mental attitude based on the wish for others to be free of their suffering. Without compassion the world would be a cruel, cold, and terrifying place to live. If there are two qualities within ourselves that human beings can really be proud of they would be compassion and love.

You Make the Difference

Having problems with your parents? Do you think they're ruining your life? Hate your brothers and sisters? What about friends? Are they giving you a hard time? There are times in our lives when all these things are true. Parents sometimes do seem to be put on this earth to give us a hard time. Siblings can be so annoying you just want to run away, and sometimes your friends can be really cruel and insensitive. The trick is to realize that you have power over how all these relationship issues affect you.

You're only a victim of relationships if you see yourself as a victim of relationships. Your mind, your perceptions about yourself, and your relationships are your most powerful weapons against the wounds of relationship hurts. It's not about steeling yourself against the world and building up walls to protect yourself, it's about seeing that you can CHOOSE to be hurt by how other people behave. It's like this: your mom has had a hard day working, shopping, cooking, and cleaning. You ask her to drop everything and take you and your friends to the movies, and she shouts back, "Okay, so you think everything revolves around you? You think I can just drop everything and run after you?" You can choose to cry, tell her you hate her, and disappear to your room. Or you can choose to say, "You're right, Mom, you've had a really hard day. I can get everyone over to watch a DVD instead." In that instance, you've not only put yourself in her shoes (and had compassion for her), you've also chosen not to take the fact that she's had a stressful day personally and come up with another way to have fun.

When you can take a step back from the immediate upset of the moment, you have POWER. And you have choice. This way of choosing to be hurt or not is incredibly liberating. It works if you're being bullied at school, arguing with your friends, being dumped by your boyfriend or girlfriend, berated by a teacher, or having a rough time with your parents.

Don't be afraid to take control of your reactions. Remember, life may throw punches at you, but you have the power to return the blow or simply move aside. I know which way I'd choose to go. I've never been fond of fighting.

CHAPTER NINE

Get It Together

Time to make the **most** of what you've got with the **ultimate guide** to looking and feeling **fab** inside and out. Get into the **GirlForce** daily **routines** and discover how to eat, rest, and play to balance your **Body Type**.

Wondering how to put everything you've learned together? Here's the lowdown on how to whip your body, mind, and spirit into shape so you can kick back and enjoy just being a girl. It's simple really. You just slip a few foods, yoga moves, exercises, and spiritual practices into your daily routine and *voilà*! You're living a GirlForce kinda life. Welcome to the new you.

LET'S FACE IT, THIS LIFE IS THE ONLY LIFE YOU'VE GOT. It may not be exactly how you wish it to be yet, but you owe it to yourself, as well as the rest of the world, to make it the best life you can possibly have. When you live in harmony with your nature, your unique Body Type, you live in a way that heals the planet. GirlForce flows outward from your body and being and into the world when you design your life to include GirlForce-boosting practices.

My GirlForce philosophy functions on two levels. On the superficial level, it's a practical guide that provides easy, get-healthy ideas and techniques. But at its core it's a spiritual and awareness practice that encourages you to take up the challenge of living more consciously, with a deep and unbreakable connection to GirlForce—the superpowered energy that makes you YOU.

How you use the GirlForce philosophy is entirely up to you! You can simply take little bits and pieces from the more practical things like the yoga moves or food suggestions or you can choose to use the philosophy as a way to connect to your spirit and get in touch with GirlForce—the magical power within. No matter how you decide to use my GirlForce philosophy, you can be sure that even the small changes you make to your life will help bring greater balance, awareness, and health to your existence.

This chapter is designed to help you put together a daily routine that will work for you. The idea here is not to shock your body and mind with a total overhaul that is impossible to sustain, but to implement change gradually, gracefully, and easily.

Daily Routines

Before you decide the whole idea of a daily routine is a total bore (especially you Air girls!), just listen up. This program isn't meant to be hard or serious. It's about having fun, sharing cool stuff with your friends and family, eating, exercising, and meditating right for your Type and ending up with a positive vibe, and a hot bod to match. The idea is to create a better-than-ever you.

Your most awesome self can be revealed in next to no time. By adding daily get-well practices, you'll discover a new fab YOU.

How It Works

Use the Daily Routines as a guide, not a boot camp–style regime. There are feel-good tips, affirmations, yoga moves, meditations, pampering practices, and dietary suggestions noted (that have been explained throughout the book), so you can be flexible about your lifestyle.

And a note on the food: the food combinations suggested are meant as a guide to the kinds of foods that will balance your Body Type. They do not take into account dietary preferences or cultural differences. The reason this book does not supply recipes and menus is so that you can adapt the food selections given in Chapter Three—Eat Right for Your Body Type—for your specific tastes and lifestyle, as well your family needs and cultural heritage. You do not have to follow any of the food suggestions; they are merely there to demonstrate a healthy, Body Type balancing way to eat. Okay?

Morning	Get up and begin the day with a calming ritual such as the affirmation: "I honor and accept myself exactly as I am."
6:00–7:00 a.m.	Do Body Type balancing yoga followed by OM meditation (about 30 minutes total). Take a warm shower or bath with five drops of essential oils, such as frankincense, jasmine, sandalwood, patchouli, chamomile, or rose. Follow with a self-massage using a nourishing body lotion. Dress yourself in colors that bring harmony and balance to your mind and Body Type: gold, yellow, pale green, blue, indigo, and brown.
7:00–8:00 a.m.	Body Type balancing breakfast: cooled, soft, moist, cooked mixed grains with soaked raisins, raw honey, papaya, banana, and sweet yogurt. If you're hungry, add an egg on multigrain toast with butter. Drink a glass of fresh fruit juice, such as apricot or apple juice.
8:00–12:00 p.m.	Activity and school time. Attend classes and communicate with others. Mid-morning snack: a cup of lemongrass herbal tea or green tea with a piece of fruit or a handful of almonds.
12:00–1:00 p.m.	Body Type balancing lunch: warm beef and veggie soup for lunch or a chicken and avocado sandwich; a piece of sweet fruit, such as a banana or peach; a handful of nuts; and a glass of fruit juice. Eat in a peaceful and calm setting. Do not sit in a cold draft.
1:00–2:00 p.m.	On the weekend: take a light nap or alternatively do some gentle yoga stretches. If you're at school, don't be afraid to take a minute to relax during study hall or a moment of free time. Be quiet and still or listen to the sound of the birds outside.
2.00–4.00 p.m.	Activity and school time.
4:00–4:30 p.m.	Afternoon snack time: make sure you rest and have a cup of herbal tea, a whole grain muffin, and a piece of fruit. Unwind from the school day.
4:30–6:30 p.m.	Homework.
6:30–7:00 p.m.	Do the Sacred Clearing Visualization for 20 minutes in a warm room.
7:00–8:00 p.m.	Body Type balancing dinner with friends and family: fresh fish with mashed sweet potato; warm green bean salad with squash, tomato, and pine nuts with olive oil dressing; and a glass of apple juice. Dessert: mango with sweet vanilla custard.
8:00–9:30 p.m.	Time to chill: read an inspiring book or listen to soothing music.
9:30–10.00 p.m.	Wind down and get ready for bed.
10:00 p.m.	Go to bed.

Air Daily Routine

Morning	Get up and begin the day with a calming ritual, such as the affirmation: "I am open to others and I accept their love and appreciation freely."
6:00–7:30 a.m.	Do some Body Type balancing exercise, like going for a swim or a light walk in a park for 20 minutes, or Body Type balancing yoga followed by OM meditation (about 30 minutes total). Take a cool to warm shower or bath with five drops of essential oils, such as ylang-ylang, peppermint, lavender, or tea tree oil. Follow with a self-massage using a soothing body lotion. Get dressed in colors that bring balance and harmony to your body and mind: pale aqua, green, pink, white, and navy blue.
7:30–8:30 a.m.	Body Type balancing breakfast: fruit salad with watermelon, figs, grapes, sweet berries, pears, oranges, and pineapple topped with ground nuts and maple syrup; and a piece of toast with avocado and cottage cheese. Drink a glass of fresh fruit juice, such as pear juice.
8:30–12:00 p.m.	Activity and school time. Communicate with others, making sure you remain even-tempered and nonaggressive. Mid-morning snack: cool, fresh juice, such as watermelon, or a piece of fruit and a milk drink.
12:00–1:00 p.m.	Body Type balancing lunch: salad sandwich, fresh fruit, a handful of nuts, and a glass of apple juice. Eat in a peaceful, quiet setting away from the heat of the midday sun. Take a stroll around a shaded garden. Now's a good time to be creative and gentle as Fire Types can experience a post-lunch energy low.
1:00–4:00 p.m.	Activity and school time.
4:00–4:30 p.m.	Afternoon snack time: a piece of fruit, a cup of green tea, and ice cream.
4:30–6:30 p.m.	Homework.
6:30–7:00 p.m.	Time to reflect on the day. It is important for Fire Types to assess the successes of the day. If you did not meditate in the morning, do the OM meditation for 20 minutes in a cool, not cold, room. If you did meditate, go for a gentle stroll around the block.
7:00–8:00 p.m.	Body Type balancing dinner with friends and family: fish and rice with steamed vegetables, including beets, carrots, Chinese broccoli, snow peas, and a dipping sauce made from soy sauce, honey, a dash of lemon, and olive oil; and a large bowl of chick pea salad with asparagus, cucumber, olives, and zucchini with ginger and walnut oil dressing. Dessert: prunes in their juice with vanilla ice cream.
8:00–9:00 p.m.	Time to chill: read something funny or listen to romantic music.
9:00–10:00 p.m.	Wind down and give thanks for the day.
10:00 p.m.	Go to bed.

Fire Daily Routine

Morning	Get up and begin the day with a stimulating ritual, such as the affirmation: "I am filled with energy and life. I am perfect just the way I am."
6:00–7:30 a.m.	Do Body Type balancing exercise, like going for a run, playing tennis or squash, or going to a circuit class at the gym for about 40 minutes. Take a warm shower or bath with five drops of essential oils, such as orange, bergamot, or grapefruit. Follow with self-massage using an invigorating body lotion. Get dressed in colors that bring balance to the body and mind: red, gold, purple, orange, and white.
7:30–8:30 a.m.	Body Type balancing breakfast: cooked and slightly warm poached fruit, plums, prunes, strawberries, and peaches with goat's milk yogurt and a little honey to sweeten. Drink a cup of chai or green tea.
8:30–12:00 p.m.	Activity and school time. Communicate with others. Mid-morning snack: a cup of mixed vegetable juice or miso soup.
12:00–1:00 p.m.	Body Type balancing lunch: spicy polenta with cooled roasted vegetables, broccoli, peppers, artichoke, carrots, cauliflower with mango chutney; dried figs with a handful of pumpkin seeds; and a glass of cranberry juice. Eat in a peaceful and calm setting. Do not sit in a cold or damp environment.
1.00–4.00 p.m.	Activity and school time.
4:00–4:30 p.m.	Afternoon snack time: chopped fresh ginger in hot water, roasted sunflower seeds, and an oatmeal cookie. Take a mindfulness break, such as focusing on the food you are eating.
4:30–6:30 p.m.	Homework.
6:30–7:00 p.m.	Do Body Type balancing yoga and follow with OM meditation (about 20 minutes total).
7:00–8:00 p.m.	Body Type balancing dinner with friends and family: baked trout with lemon and thyme; steamed vegetables, such as green beans, asparagus, beets, and corn. Dessert: cooked fruit salad with sago pudding and a glass of cherry juice.
8:00–9:00 p.m.	Take time to chill: read an inspiring book or listen to calming music.
9:00–10:00 p.m.	Get ready for bed and give thanks for the day.
10:00 p.m.	Go to bed.

Earth Daily Routine

What to Add to Your Daily Life for All Body Types

It's hard enough getting through school, navigating the complexities of friendships and dating, coming to grips with a changing body, and dealing with fluctuating emotions without having to figure out what to eat or how to exercise. That's where I can help. The Daily Routines are designed to be goof-proof. They're meant to take the "hard work" out of being healthy and staying in balance. And you can do them by taking baby steps.

Here are some tips that will help all the three Body Types stay in balance and help you put your own routine together. Take what you like from the list and let go of the rest. Again, the idea is to take stress out of your life, not add to it—so go easy and do what feels good.

1. Go for foods that are Right for Your Body Type. 2. Go for exercise that's Right for Your Body Type. 3. Work on stress-management strategies that are Right for Your Body Type. 4. Do meditation practices. 5. Do yoga routines that are Right for Your Body Type. 6. Pamper yourself with self-massage using essential oils that are Right for Your Body Type. 7. Wear clothes and colors that are Right for Your Body Type. 8. Eat more organic foods. 9. Do the Sacred Clearing Visualization. 10. Book sessions with counselors when you need them. 11. Food meditations—think about what you put in your mouth. 12. Self-nurturing activities—the more you can include self-pampering and nurturing activities in your daily life, the better you will feel about yourself and your world. Anything that YOU consider to be fun, blissful, joyful, playful, exciting, relaxing, enjoyable, stimulating, pleasurable, sensuous, or nourishing will heal you by boosting your GirlForce.

What to Ditch from Your
Daily Life for All Body Types

1. Self-punishment 2. Processed foods 3. Too much television 4. Too much work 5. Cigarettes, recreational drugs, and alcohol 6. Negative self-talk 7. Pollution 8. Abuse and violence of any kind 9. Guilt 10. Poor body image

Go for It, Girl!

By now you've probably worked out that GirlForce offers an amazing way to live and feel. It's not just about having a hot body or clear skin, it's about feeling great about who you are. And while you were born with a ready supply of babelicious GirlForce energy, you can pump up the volume on that supply by adding the suggestions outlined in the Daily Routines into your life. GirlForce is an empowering way to live because it gives you permission to be yourself, make your own choices and be in tune with your own nature. Give me more!

Remember, GirlForce is all about adding in ideas, rituals, food, and exercises gently. Don't force anything; don't beat yourself up if the suggestions seem impossible to you. Set your own pace that works in with your lifestyle, family, schedule, and culture, and go easy on yourself. GirlForce only works when you stress down, not out.

CHAPTER TEN

Your GirlForce Questions Answered

The secret of **GirlForce** is understanding you're **perfect just as you are**. You have your own special look, **personality**, and **abilities**, which are totally unique to you. When you **stop worrying** whether you should be more like someone else, you'll totally own the power of **GirlForce**.

You're about to delve into the GirlForce Q&A chapter, where all those uncomfortable questions such as "Why have all my friends got boobs while I'm flat as a pancake?" or "Am I the only one in the world daydreaming constantly about my crush?" are answered. Knowing your Body Type will also help explain lots of the weird and wonderful things that make you who you are.

OKAY, LET'S BE HONEST, who doesn't compare themselves to their friends? It's perfectly natural for chicks to compare themselves. We all look in the mirror and check out bits of our bodies and compare them to our friends' shapes and sizes. Problems arise when we look in the mirror and let a barrage of insults fly at our faces, bodies, skin, personality, anything you can think of. Not everyone is so extreme, but many girls don't like the way they look and feel, and get really down on themselves. Some of the bad feelings can be blamed on hormones, some on poor self-esteem, peer and family issues, and some on the media (which constantly tells us there's only one look, one body shape, one style that's attractive). Some of the blame for feeling down about ourselves also has to fall on our own shoulders. There's a moment in every girl's life when we have to say, "Enough is enough! I'm sick of feeling not okay about myself, and I'm going to do something about it!" The fact that you're reading this book is an affirmation that you want to master feeling totally fab, sassy, and cool!

This Q&A section won't answer all your questions about how to handle growing up, and I want to say again I'm not a doctor or counselor, but I hope it will cover loads of things that you really want answered from an Ayurvedic perspective. Read them, then make up your own mind about whether they relate to you or not.

The World's Most
Embarrassing Questions

Q: Why is everyone in my group developing boobs at a different rate?

A: On the whole, curvy Earth girls tend to develop larger breasts than their athletic Fire and more petite Air girlfriends. Earth girls also tend to develop breasts and sprout pubic hair before the Air and Fire girls. Air girls, who can be either very tall or petite, can also develop large breasts, but most often Air girls develop smaller breasts than the other two Body Types. Fire girls generally have medium-sized breasts. Many girls freak out that their boobs are too small or too big during puberty, but it's good to remember that your breasts will continue to develop throughout your teens. Once you stop growing, you'll discover that your overall body proportions have changed and, therefore, your breasts may finally look right in relation to your shape and size. The best advice is to try to accept your body shape and size as it is. Don't compare yourself unfavorably to your friends. Just know that you're a beautiful and perfect expression of nature and GirlForce no matter what size your breasts are.

Q: Why have some of my friends got their periods and some haven't?

A: Of course, there are no hard and fast rules here, but generally speaking Earth girls are often the first to get their periods, followed by Fire, while Air girls are generally the last to hit puberty. Many girls sail through their monthly cycles, barely registering a blip on the physical or emotional radar. But there are also plenty of girls who experience the odd problem around period time; from little breakouts and cramps to feeling a bit down in the dumps. Your Body Type will explain quite a lot about the way you experience your periods.

Air girls often have light and irregular periods. Sometimes the color of the blood is darkish-red and can be accompanied by cramps and lower back pain and headaches. Air girls can feel a bit blue around period time, and sometimes they can also feel anxious and have difficulty getting to sleep. Don't worry if your period also comes with a little constipation; it's also common for Air girls to get a bit bloated around this time. The best way to treat any menstrual irregularities is to follow the Daily Routines for the Air Body Type and ensure that you go to bed early, rest, and do very little exercise during the first couple of days of the monthly flow. Fire girls sometimes have an excessive menstrual flow. The blood can be dark or very red and it can be hot and profuse. The period is sometimes associated with a fever along with flushed skin and red eyes. Skin rashes and acne can occur, as well as mild diarrhea. Fire girls can also get irritated during this time. If you experience any of these symptoms, try to stick to the Daily Routines for the Fire Body Type and make sure you rest, eat cooling foods, and don't get too hot under the collar during this phase of your cycle. Earth girls have a moderate flow but the period typically lasts longer than Air or Fire girls. The blood may be pale and light red with a slow but continuous flow. Sometimes the period is accompanied by feelings of heaviness and tiredness. Often Earth girls will get some breast tenderness, and a little bloating and water retention. If you experience these symptoms, follow the Earth Body Type Daily Routines, make sure you rest (although don't go to bed), and drink stimulating ginger tea to help flush the system.

Whatever Body Type you are, if you experience any extreme symptoms with your period, such as excessive cramping, back pain, severe acne, extreme mood swings, very light flow or very heavy flow, go see your doctor.

Q: Yuck, I've got body odor. Why me?
A: Your hormones account for a large part of the changes in your body, even your scent, but your Body Type also plays a role in the way your body smells. This may be embarrassing, but it's helpful to know that it's perfectly natural for different Body Types to have quite different odors. Fire girls can often have very strong-smelling feet and armpits that put out an acrid odor, which sometimes won't disappear even after washing. Air Types tend to have less body odor than the other two types because they perspire less, and Earth types can sometimes have a slightly metallic, sweet odor (especially around period time). The best way to keep all body odors to a minimum is to have a consistently healthy diet and exercise routine. A happy, functioning digestive system will help you eliminate toxins from your body, and regular exercise and yoga will speed the digestive processes. Treat yourself to regular aromatherapy baths, using essential oils such as lavender and tea tree, which have cleansing actions on the skin (they're antifungal, antibacterial, and antiseptic) and they banish unpleasant BO. If you need to use a deodorant, go for a natural one from the health food store that doesn't contain any harsh chemicals. And a little spritz of perfume before you walk out the door each day goes a long way too.

Q: Why do I daydream about my crush all the time?
A: Daydream about Orlando Bloom or Johnny Depp? Maybe you have a crush on someone in your class? Everyone fantasizes about kissing their favorite boys (and sometimes girls) at some point. That said, Air girls tend to fantasize more than Fire and Earth girls do. Air girls are prone to having complex daydreams while Fire girls tend to have fantasies that involve challenge and competition, and Earth girls have dreamy, romantic fantasies. Of course, you can be an Earth babe and still dream about hunting down the hottie from your science class or you can be an Air girl and not be interested in boys (or girls) at all—there are no universal truths when it comes to your sexuality. We are all different and have different dreams and passions. Don't beat yourself up about your romantic desires. It's perfectly natural for you to think about crushes and romance a lot, or not at all. Take the "shoulds" and "oughts" out of your internal dialogue and let yourself experience the changes in your body and mind as they occur naturally.

Q: Why aren't I interested in sex when everyone else seems to be?
A: Even though Earth girls tend to get breasts, hips, and pubic hair before their Air and Fire friends, of all the Body Types, Earth girls tend to be the last to become interested in sex. Their relaxed, slow and steady approach to life also translates into a fairly laid-back approach to sex. Often Earth girls can have a take-it-or-leave-it approach, which, when compared to Air's intense desires and Fire's passionate wants, seems a bit lukewarm. Air Types, who tend to develop physically later than Fire and Earth girls, may also be slower to become interested in sex than Fire girls. That said, Air Types have active

imaginations and may start fantasizing about sex and relationships in their early teens. Fire Types, who are generally quite confident, are usually the first in the group to develop passionate, flaming desires, which can occur early in their teens.

The key is to be aware of your own needs and desires and not let anyone push you beyond your limits. When it comes to sex "No always means NO." You won't lose your cred if you are firm about your boundaries with your friends and boyfriends. If anything, your friends will respect you for asserting your needs and limits.

From an Ayurvedic standpoint, sexual desires will generally not occur until you are physically and emotionally ready. Ayurveda recommends that girls should not push themselves (ever) into sexual encounters until they feel mature enough to handle the consequences, which can be pretty heavy, such as pregnancy, sexually transmitted diseases, and stress. It's good common sense to hang back (even if all your friends are having sex) until you feel it's cool for you to engage in a loving partnership. According to Ayurveda, having sex before you're ready creates a lot of stress, which is bad for all Body Types.

Q: Why is my skin breaking out?

A: All three Body Types can get zits during puberty. Earth Types tend to get blackheads and deep, oily pustules; Air types have small pores and tend to get tiny blackheads around the T-zone; and Fire girls can get angry, sore red acne and rashes anywhere on the face, back, and occasionally on the chest. Fire gals, who are constitutionally a bit hot, tend to get rashes and skin breakouts more readily than Earth or Air girls. Most acne settles down after puberty (which doesn't help much while you're enduring the hell

of skin eruptions), but while you're going through breakout cycles there's a lot you can do to calm the skin and keep it free from zits (check out Chapter Five).

Q: Alcohol and drugs, are they okay?

A: By the time you're reading this, you've probably been exposed on some level to drugs and alcohol. Maybe your parents drink wine with dinner? Maybe someone you know smokes cigarettes? Whether you've been exposed to drugs and alcohol or not, at some point you will be offered drugs and alcohol. Your parents will have their own attitudes to the intake of these substances, but from a GirlForce point of view it's never okay to get out of it or out of control. Why? Because by the time you feel drunk, stoned, or high your body has had to work overtime to process a heap of chemicals. In girls, the chemical called alcohol dehydrogenase, an enzyme that breaks down alcohol in the stomach, is a lot less effective than it is in boys, which is why girls get drunk faster on less alcohol than boys. Even in small amounts your liver, kidneys, and brain are affected by the alcohol.

Drugs and alcohol also compromise your ability to make clearheaded choices—whether or not to get into a car with other intoxicated kids, whether or not to have sex with someone, or whether or not to take harder drugs or drink more alcohol. When you trash yourself with alcohol and drugs your GirlForce goes way down. With a drug or alcohol hangover you feel sick, depleted, and tired and you're less likely to do the things that lift your GirlForce, such as doing your yoga or exercise routines. And don't think smoking is okay because it doesn't get you high. It won't kill you— now—but it's one of the leading causes of death in our society and it's highly addictive. I know many people may think the damage smoking can do seems too far in the future to care about, so if you can't wrap your head around the diseases associated with smoking, think about how your mouth, hair, and skin will smell like an ashtray, your fingers and nails will turn yellow from the nicotine, and imagine the wrinkles you'll get. Gross!

It's unlikely that you'll become *instantly* addicted to alcohol or drugs such as pot (heroine, cocaine, crack, and speed are other issues), but it's not really the point. Taking drugs of any kind has serious side effects, some of which can be really dangerous for your mind, body, and spirit. This is not about being preachy, it's about being aware that all your choices have consequences.

If you want more info on different drugs and how they affect you, head to the National Institute of Drug Abuse Web site at www.nida.nih.gov.

Q: I'm so moody I can go through highs and lows in one day. Why?

A: Right now your hormones are raging and they're playing havoc with your moods and emotions. Most teens feel they are on an emotional roller-coaster. Your Body Type will also influence how you deal with your moods and emotions. Air babes tend to be a bit nervous and anxious, and they're the ones most likely to have extreme mood swings from deliriously happy to really down. When Fire divas are up, they're motivated and focused, but when they're blue, they're irritable and aggressive. Earth gals tend to be the most even-keeled of all the Types, but when they're out of sync, they can become withdrawn and sullen. The best way to keep your moods in check, whatever Body Type you are, is to maintain a balanced body, mind, and spirit. And you know how to do that! Just eat, exercise, meditate, dress, perform yoga

postures, and beautify according to your Body Type. When you take conscious steps to stay in balance every day, your moods will stabilize and you'll be less likely to be at the mercy of your hormones.

It's important to recognize the difference between being moody and being depressed. About one out of every five teens is suffering from some sort of serious depression. And given that depression is the biggest cause of youth suicide, it's important to discover the difference between being in a bit of a slump (because of school, family, or other pressures) and being depressed. Sadly, only 20 percent of teens with depression ever seek proper help or advice. Don't be one of those suffering in silence. If you recognize any or all of these symptoms seek immediate medical advice.

- Thoughts of death or suicide
- Feelings of helplessness
- No energy
- Serious mood swings
- Poor concentration
- Insomnia
- Oversleeping
- No interest in life
- Extreme weight gain or weight loss

Q: I'm being bullied at school. What should I do?

A: It doesn't matter if you're tall, short, big, or small, bullying can happen to anyone who appears different from the rest of the crowd. Bullies usually target people they think are different from themselves. These differences might be gender, culture, sexuality, a disability, or even the way somebody dresses or does their hair. Sometimes victims are the shy, introverted types with low self-worth (which is another good reason to work on your self-esteem) and sometimes victims of bullying are picked at random.

The experts say that most victims of bullying suffer in silence. They don't tell their teachers or their parents that they are being picked on. *The first thing you have to do if you're being verbally or physically abused is report it to your parents or your teacher.* There is no shame in not being able to handle bullying (most people can't), and it's essential to end the cycle of harm being perpetrated against you. If you are being bullied, own up to the fact that you have a problem and go and talk to a trusted adult about it—this doesn't mean you're a tattletale! Remember, you're not alone; a recent study found that 91 percent of people admit they have been bullied at some point in their lives and about 50 percent of kids say they're being picked on at school. For more information try: www.stopbullyingnow.hrsa.gov.

Q: Why do people make me feel so different?

A: We live in a harsh world that judges people on very superficial things, such as how you look, what you wear, your race, what group you belong to, where you live, what your parents do, and so on. These judgments can turn into bullying and cruelty.

Most people behave badly because they are afraid. The school bullies are sometimes the most insecure people of the group—often they pick on you to feel stronger and tougher because they feel weak inside. If you're being judged by your peers and are wondering what's wrong with you, it pays to ask yourself, "What are they afraid of?" Maybe you can't see it but perhaps they think you're smarter than they are? Or maybe they think *you've* got it all together? Maybe they're just plain jealous of you?

Being singled out and teased by a group of people can be crushing. Your best course of action is to try not to take it personally or believe their bad PR about you. One empowering way to handle the situation is to ask them straight out why they're being nasty to you. It can be incredibly scary doing this, and you may need to coax yourself into it with a few affirmations, but rather than giving your power away to them, it pays to take ownership of the situation and confront it head on. If they can't supply a satisfactory answer, move on, and try to make new friends. When you take the risk to chat with new girls, you'll find there are lots of people who feel just like you. Sign up for a sport or a dance class that has regular games or classes on weekends. There are PLUs (People Like You) out there who will like you for who you are. You just need to find them.

Q: Why do I freak out so much about exams?

A: From a Body Type perspective, Air Types are generally the ones who get the most stressed out about exams. While they're often very intelligent, they don't have great long-term memories and exams tend to be a poor representation of their talents and abilities. Also, Air girls can lie awake all night worrying about exams, so the next day they feel drained and exhausted. Even though Air girls are not overly fond of schedules and routines, they benefit a lot from doing some pre-exam preparation. Leaving it till the last minute is one sure-fire way to freak out. Work out a study plan, do a little bit at a time, take mini-breaks, and do some meditation to help calm your Air girl's nerves.

Fire Types, who are the mega-achievers of the posse, tend to feel more confident about exams, but they demand a lot of themselves—coming in last is not an option for Fire babes. Exams can excite and stimulate a Fire girl because they present an opportunity for her to reveal her skills and shine. If she hasn't done a lot of work during the year, exams can also get a Fire girl hot under the collar. Fire girls benefit when they figure out ways to stay calm and get the work done. Make a study plan. Check off the tasks as you complete them. This way you'll see you're making progress without feeling like you have to burn the midnight oil to achieve results.

Earth girls tend to procrastinate about studying. While they don't mind sitting on their butts and reading for hours on end, they would rather read a romance novel than put their nose to the grindstone. Earth girls are often dedicated and diligent students who don't find it too hard to discipline themselves to do the work. They get into trouble when their

need to please turns into tummy-churning panic about how they're going to do in exams and what their parents and peers will think if they fail. They have good memories, which serve them well in exams, so their best plan of attack is to get into it. Turn off the TV, stop procrastinating, and dive into the books. It's also important for Earth girls to break up their study periods with some stimulating exercise to get the creative juices flowing and the blood moving.

Work It, Baby

GIRLFORCE IS NOT JUST A COOL PHILOSOPHY, it's a way of life. When you add all the tools and techniques you've learned in this book to your lifestyle, you'll feel awesome. GirlForce is about following a lifestyle program, but it's also about plugging into the source of your feel-good spiritual power, your GirlForce.

In order to get an energy-boosting hit of GirlForce every day, you need to incorporate the practices into your lifestyle. You need to eat, exercise, dress, do yoga moves, and think in a way that's right for your particular Body Type. You'll get the most out of this book if you LIVE IT!

Start a diary or workbook and record your GirlForce experiences. Write down the new things you've discovered about yourself since you found out about your Body Type. Share your insights with your friends, and, if you want, start a GirlForce club where you can all get together and share ideas, swap tips, and go shopping for Body Type balancing foods, fashions, and beauty tools.

GirlForce is the power to be who you are. It's confidence. It's self-esteem. It's belief in your abilities and talents. It's knowing you're okay no matter what. It's feeling like a goddess even when you're having a bad hair day. And it's understanding that as an Air babe, a Fire chick, or an Earth angel, you are a perfect part of nature. GirlForce is about being connected to each other, as well as being cool about being yourself. GirlForce is about being compassionate with others, and it's being aware of your choices. GirlForce is a power no one can take away from you because it lives within your heart and soul.

The ONLY way to connect to the girl power within is to work it. Like a muscle, it comes alive when you pump it. Now it's time to dive into the cool world of GirlForce. Go, girl!

Acknowledgments

Many thanks to Prue Ruscoe for her fabulous photography and Gayna Murphy for her brilliant design.

A million thanks to all the wonderful models who worked so hard on the shoot: Elizabeth Green from ACM, Sarah Ash, Chris Mathews, William Horbacz from Vivien's, Eunice Ward and Emma Adams from Chadwicks, Kieta Van Ewyk from Chic, Patric Rodrigues Fernandes from SCENE, Hillary Andersen from Work, Kitty Callaghan, and Lucy Le Masurier.

Thank you to the professional stylists and hair and makeup artists who worked on the book: Pilar Pardes and Kimberley Forbes.

My deepest thanks to Bill Clark, Allison, and Liam for all their faith in *GirlForce*. I look forward to a lifetime of love and laughs with you all.

Thank you to the amazing team at Bloomsbury for believing in *GirlForce*. Special thanks to Michelle Nagler, Caroline Abbey, Deb Shapiro, and everyone else who has given their energy and special love to me and the book.

To Rowan and Liberty Jacob, my dear and loving family, you are my inspiration.

The author and publisher would like to thank the following individuals and organizations for kindly supplying their time, props, and clothing: MAC Cosmetics, Adidas, Angelique, Ashley Wilson, Bonds, Bettina Liano, Cohen et Sabine, Converse, Electric, Fabienne, Fleur Wood, Flux, George, Glassons, Gorman, IKEA, Just Jeans, Kitten, Levi's, Lovable, Lucky 13, Mambo, My Island Home, Nicola, Peter Alexander, Peter Lang, Play, Playboy, Poko Pano, Puma, Rip Curl, Ruby Star Traders, Seafolly, Seduce, Skipping Girl, Smith & Miles, Sportsgirl, Stellar, Target, Third Millennium, Tie Rack, Tree of Life, Toxic, Urban Rituelle, Zomp Shoez.